Naughty Alice

by

Cheryl Lee Latter

Copyright © 2015 Cheryl Lee Latter

Cover by Ida Jansson at Amygdala Design

All rights reserved. No part of this book may be reproduced in any form, except for the inclusion of brief quotations in review, without permission in writing from the author/publisher.

All characters and towns are fictitious. Any resemblance to people or places are purely coincidental. The WI depicted in this story is in no way affiliated with the worldwide WI of the same name.

For Eden, Alice and Nancy

Part One - Nancy

Chapter One

The Sunny Meadows village hall was filling up very nicely on this starry October evening.

Mayor Bloom stood at the front of the crowd, his whiskers fairly trembling with excitement. This was one of the few evenings of the year when he was guaranteed a good turn-out.

The villagers filed into the rows of plastic seats - more commonly put to use for Weight Watchers meetings or school plays - and made themselves comfortable. They all kept on their coats, and pulled them tightly around them against the chilly evening.

The yearly budget did not stretch to central heating in the hall.

Ten year old Nancy Bloom sat in the front row, kicking her feet and watching the breath come out of her in icy plumes. She was buttoned up tightly in a long red coat with white fur edging which squeezed her when she sat down.

The room settled down and her father stood facing them all, like a war-monger proudly inspecting his troops.

'Well,' he beamed, 'it's that time again.'

There was twittering from the spinsters in the front row, the Mayor's biggest fans.

Nancy rolled her eyes, and beside her, Mrs Bloom put a discreet hand on Nancy's knee and shook her head. She stopped kicking, but continued to watch her warm breath hit the cold air.

'November!' announced the Mayor. 'And so begins our annual entry for the county's Festive Christmas Village Competition.'

He said this with such importance, it was practically possible to hear the capital letters.

The spinster's ooh-ed, as if they didn't already know what the entire point of the meeting was. Nancy thought this was probably the highlight of their entire year. Time to knit, bake, crochet, make lists, glue tinsel to everything, and finally have use for all those paper plates they've been stockpiling all summer.

'So here we are again,' continued Mayor Bloom, his cheeks rosy with pride. 'Five time winners in the Winter Wonderland section, four time winners in the Christmas Bake Extravaganza - thanks, of course, to our own Mrs Twigg'. Cue the good Mrs Twigg blushing up to the carnations on her hat, along with much cooing and nudging of her friends. 'And, of course, gold award and overall winners of River County's Best Festive Christmas Village *three years running*!'

There was a fine splattering of applause from the audience. Nancy wondered if her father would point out that these were the same three years he had been Mayor, but decided that even he wouldn't be so obvious.

'Might I add, these are the same three years that you good people have been kind enough to call me your Mayor!' boomed Mayor Bloom.

Nancy shook her head in disappointment. She squirmed in her coat and tried to undo a few buttons, but her mother looked at her with pursed lips until she sat still.

Looking around the room, she caught little Joey Litten looking at her. He pulled a grotesque face at her. Nancy pulled an even uglier one back. Joey screwed up his face and used his fingers to pull the sides of his mouth open and stuck out his tongue. Joey's mother spotted him and batted him with the back of her hand until he stopped.

Nancy sniggered and turned back to the front, pretending not to notice her mother's disapproving look. She smiled sweetly at her father, as though she was rapt by his words, not that he was looking her way.

'This year will be the biggest yet,' he continued. 'The county has announced that this years' winner, as well as being the envy of all other villages, from Northbridge to Weasel Pass, shall win the glorious amount of £50,000 to be spent as the villagers choose.'

There were excited exclamations from the crowd, as they immediately began to mentally spend so much money.

Mayor Bloom bathed in the response from his announcement. 'Who knows,' he said, 'what we could do with such money? More flowers for the Village Horticultural Society' - murmurs from the men - 'or a large investment into my own village golf course plans' - groans from the women - 'or even just a huge party for all of us!' - cheers from the men and women alike.

'I would say that judging from our previous record, that win is in the bag. And that is why I say now that Sunny Meadows will deliver the biggest, the brightest, the snowiest, the sparkliest, the most traditional, reindeer-filled, eggnog-flowing, jingle bells jingling, fabulously fun and festive Christmas the judges have ever seen!'

There were cheers and applause from the villagers.

'Great,' muttered Nancy.

It was bad enough being the daughter of the Mayor the rest of the year, but it was quite unbearable in winter. In the Bloom household, talk of Christmas began in October, and ended sometime in mid-January. She had grown to hate every minute of it.

After the meeting, everyone milled around by the doorway for a while. Nancy stood by waiting for her parents as they socialised and talked excited plans.
A group of girls from the primary school played tag on the grass, squealing and shouting, happy to be out late and to see friends for play in the dark.
Nancy watched them from the door. They looked so happy and free, running on the grass with rosy cheeks and bright laughter.
She tugged at Mrs Bloom's sleeve. 'Mother, can I go and play?'
'No, darling, of course not.'
Mrs Bloom returned to her conversation, forgetting about her.
One of the girls saw Nancy watching and smiled at her. Nancy smiled back, and took a step towards her, onto the grass.
'Nancy, come back here! You'll ruin your shoes.'
Nancy looked down at her shiny black shoe on the dry grass, and frowned. She stepped back onto the path.

In the limousine on the way to dinner, Nancy squirmed in her coat while her parents told Chester, the driver, about the village's plans. Nancy was sure that Chester didn't care in the slightest, but he was doing a good job of pretending.
'Mother, may I take off my coat?'
'Of course not, dear.'

She looked out of the window. they were leaving Sunny Meadows on the way to Gardenia Heights. There they would sit in a fabulous restaurant eating lobster and new potatoes and drinking expensive bottled water. And they would congratulate themselves on being rich and powerful and in charge.

Nancy hated lobster.

She looked at the houses they were passing, houses in which other people lived other lives. She wondered what it would be like to be one of them.

After a while, the houses got fewer and fewer, and all she could see was darkness and trees.

'And that, my dear Chester, is why we will win again!' beamed her father.

There was a ratcheting screech and the car spluttered a few times, then stopped.

'What is it, Chester?' said Mrs Bloom, worried.

'I'm not sure,' said Chester. He tried to start up the car, but nothing happened. He pulled out his mobile phone and tried to use it. 'No signal, either.'

Her parents pulled out their own phones and tapped at them. 'No signal,' said her father. He never took other peoples' word for things. If someone told him it was five o'clock, he would look at his watch rather than just believe them.

'There's a garage not far away,' said Chester. 'In Hogweed Fields, on the outskirts. Probably take me about half an hour to walk.'

'You're not going to just leave us here?' said Mrs Bloom.

'Nothing else for it,' said the Mayor. 'Take the torch, Chester.'

'I'll get help.'

Chester got out of the warm car and headed off into the frosty night.

The three Blooms sat for a while in the car, waiting for help. Soon Nancy got restless and lay down in her seat.

'Sit up, dear, you'll rumple your dress.'

Nancy sat up. 'Can I get out of the car?'

'No, of course not.'

'Actually,' said her father, surprising them all, 'let's all get out.'

Her mother put a hand on his arm. 'Horatio, it might not be safe.'

'Nonsense,' Veronica,' he said, wonderingly. 'I know this place. I know it very well.'

He stepped out of the car, and Nancy shrugged and scrambled out after him. Her mother watched them from the door.

Nancy followed her father into the road. It was a wide open space, lit by a bright moon. The car had stalled at a crossroads, four plain white roads forking off into different directions.

Nancy looked at the signposts. One led to Gardenia Heights, one to the city thirty miles away, the one they were on led back to Sunny Meadows, and the final one led to Hogweed Fields.

Nancy knew about Hogweed Fields. It was everything that Sunny Meadows was not.

The people in Hogweed Fields didn't have much money. Nancy's father had told her several times that this was because no-one tried to do better. There was no community, no village choir, no garden fetes in the summer months. Nancy had heard that the high school was full of rough children who fought and swore.

The outskirts of the two villages met, and Nancy and her school friends had been brought up knowing not to cross the boundary line.

Now her father looked misty-eyed as he looked down the road where Chester's torchlight had long since disappeared into the darkness.

'Did I ever tell you,' asked the Mayor of Sunny Meadows, wistfully, 'that I grew up in Hogweed Fields?'

Nancy was surprised. 'You?'

'Oh, yes. My family actually ran the garage at the end of this road. My dad wanted me to stay with him, to take over the family business.'

Nancy stood with her mouth open. The idea of her father being the friendly local mechanic was impossible to imagine. He was so utterly *Mayor-like*.

'I wanted more,' said her father. 'I was named after a great leader, you know - Lord Horatio Nelson. I felt that the world had much grander things to offer me than to spend my days changing spark plugs and living on the poverty line. I worked hard - I had my first job when I was 12 years old, delivering newspapers. I saved my money, and then I worked my way through university. I was the first one in my family to get an education.'

Nancy was still struggling with the image of her dad being poor. He looked so at home in their plush sitting room, or at their highly-polished dining table, dabbing red wine from his thick moustache. She couldn't imagine him as a child, delivering newspapers on his bicycle in the rain to earn a few meagre pennies.

'I worked every night and went to classes every day,' said her father. 'But it wasn't enough.'

'What happened?' asked Nancy.

'I failed spectacularly,' said the Mayor, simply. 'I didn't get my degree, I lost my job, and I had to move out of my student flat. I had nothing left. I hitchhiked most of the way home. A kind man on his way from the city to Gardenia Heights dropped me at this crossroads.'

A cloud passed across the moon, plunging them into darkness.

'I had a decision to make,' said Mayor Bloom. 'To go home in shame and ask my father for a job, or to try again. I spent the night right here, beside the road. In the morning, I stood in the middle, where the roads meet. I decided to let Fate make the decision for me.'

Nancy was wide-eyed. 'What did you do?'

'I closed my eyes, and I turned in circles, three, four times. I decided to head down the road I was facing, wherever it led.'

'And it led you to Sunny Meadows?' whispered Nancy.

The cloud passed and out came the moon, lighting up her father's face as he smiled down at her.

'It did,' he said. 'The first thing I did was go into the nearest coffee shop. I had enough money for a hot drink to toast my new start. And that day, I met your mother. She was my waitress.'

Nancy looked in shock at her mother, sitting half in and half out of the car. *A waitress?* She assumed her mother had never worked in her life.

'So, you see, Nancy, things could have been so different. If I'd have taken another path, I never would have met your mother, and we never would have got you. I'd have met another wife, and maybe another girl would have been born.'

Nancy thought of another girl. Her, but not her. 'What do you mean, you got me?'

The Mayor waved a dismissive hand. 'Oh, you know what I mean. Just a figure of speech.'

He put his arm around her and squeezed her shoulder, as a dim light appeared on the horizon, heading toward them.

'It's cold, and here comes help. Let's go back to the car.'

Chapter Two

Mrs Veronica Bloom's coffee mornings were famous in the village.

She always had the cleanest linen tablecloths, the shiniest teapots, and the nicest cakes. Mrs Bloom turned up her nose at shop-bought cakes and pastries. All of hers were strictly home-made. Not by her, of course, but by Millie, the housekeeper. No-one needed to know that, though. Mrs Bloom didn't lie, exactly. She just let people believe what they wanted to.

Nancy enjoyed the cakes, but not so much the conversation. She sat politely in her shiny shoes, and tried to eat as much as possible without drawing attention to herself.

The famed Mrs Twigg often brought a cake or two of her own, or a new bottle of elderflower cordial. Purely out of generosity, you see, and not at all in an attempt to upstage her hostess.

The women spoke of their plans to make plans to hold a coffee morning to make other plans. (Why not just talk about it now? thought Nancy, as she always did).

Eventually there was a lull in the conversation, and as always, someone filled it by turning to Nancy.

'How are your studies going, Nancy?' asked Mrs Blatch, a large woman who crocheted all her own hats.

'Fine, thank you,' said Nancy, sweetly.

'Didn't you want to go to school with your friends?' asked Mrs Mouse, an unfortunately-named woman with an unusually pointed nose.

Nancy opened her mouth, but Mrs Bloom answered for her, 'Luckily, we are able to give Nancy the best private tuition around. Millicent is worth her weight in gold. She does so much around the house, without even being asked.'

Like baking for your dreaded coffee mornings, thought Nancy, sulkily biting into a pink macaroon. She would have loved the chance to go to school, but her parents thought she was too good for that.

'I don't have any friends,' Nancy blurted out.

The ladies seemed embarrassed.

'Oh, I'm sure you do,' said portly Mrs Harriet. 'You must.'

'I don't.'

'She's just being dramatic,' said Mrs Bloom. 'She has lots of friends. Like Carrie-Ann and Marguerite.'

Nancy scowled. Carrie-Ann and Marguerite were what she thought of as her parent-approved friends. For years they had been pushed together for play-dates and sleepovers and wholesome activities. None of them got along, though, and their enforced hours together were not fun.

'I do remember something,' said Nancy.

Mrs Blatch smiled, indulgently.

'I remember Alice.'

The women looked at her, quietly.

'Naughty Alice. She was my imaginary friend.'

Nancy turned to her mother.

'Don't you remember?' she said. 'When I was a little girl, whenever I did anything wrong, I would say, "it wasn't me - it was Alice", and poor Alice took the blame for everything.'

Mrs Blatch laughed. 'An imaginary friend.'

'My name is Nancy Alice Bloom,' explained Nancy. 'She looked just like me.'

'Her grandmothers names on her father's side,' explained Mrs Bloom. 'They died long before she was born.'

The ladies tittered with friendly laughter, but Nancy frowned.

'So, is Alice still with us,' Mrs Blatch asked Nancy. 'Or do you just not do naughty things anymore?' She grinned over her teacup.

'Nancy is a good girl,' said Mrs Bloom, proudly. 'We've raised her with a firm hand. I've always said if you keep a child busy, they won't have the time or the inclination to get into mischief.'

Nancy the good girl smiled nicely at her mother and the other ladies, and they smiled nicely back.

The Blooms lived in a beautiful Manor house. It was large and white and square and symmetrical. It was everything Mr and Mrs Bloom approved of. Before Mr Bloom became Mayor, they lived in a similar house, just small and white and square and symmetrical. Nancy often wondered if her parents would be happier if she was square and symmetrical, too.

Nancy had a lovely bedroom, the kind of bedroom most girls would dream of.

She had a huge bed with fluffy bedding and lots of high pillows. The walls were pale and floral and pinkish. The furniture was antique, with ornate handles and mirrors with carved frames.

She had her own bathroom with a claw-foot spa bath and thick pink towels and lavender soaps, and a dressing room of her own. Nancy didn't really think a child needed a dressing room, unless it was full of toys and dressing-up clothes.

Nancy liked her room, which had large picture windows looking over the garden. She liked lying on her bed with the curtains open, watching the dawn sunlight, watching the blossoms drift from the trees, watching the starlit clouds blow across the sky.

Still, she never felt like it was truly her own room. The furniture came with the house, so although it was lovely, it wasn't really her style. Her mother chose the clothes in the wardrobes and the books on the shelf and the textbooks on the desk. She wasn't allowed to put pictures on the walls in case it ruined the antique wallpaper, and the pink towels in the bathroom were a colour she hated. She didn't understand why green towels would make a difference to anyone but her.

Before bed that night, Nancy sat cross-legged in her white nightdress in front of her floor-length mirror and brushed out her thick blonde hair.

She looked closely at her reflection while she did it.

'Alice,' she whispered, and stared at her face to see if it changed. 'Naughty Alice.'

She stared and stared. After a while, she felt that the look in her eyes had changed, but maybe it was just her imagination.

It was like when you say a familiar word over and over again until it turns into just a meaningless sound.

Nancy thought it was the same with faces. If you look at your own face for long enough, stare into your own eyes, eventually it looks different to you, like the face of someone you vaguely recognise, but a stranger.

Even though it was only mid-November, the shops were beginning to fill up with Christmas items and carols were already heard here and there throughout the mall.

Nancy enjoyed the glitter and glitz. Even though she wasn't a little child anymore, she still let herself get caught up in the excitement and magic of this time of year.

She trailed along behind her mother, wrapped in a coat with a fluffy hood, even though it was unseasonably warm out, and certainly warm inside.

Veronica Bloom veered ahead, greeting everyone she knew, but making sure not to stop for too much conversation. She carried shiny store bags, all red and white with snowflakes and silver shapes on the front of them.

Nancy stopped for a moment to look at a display. It was a fake garden, with a snowman and a little reindeer smiling in fake snow. 'Frosty The Snowman' played from somewhere within it. Two toy children held snowballs, their mechanical hands moving back and forth with the music, but never throwing anything. She watched the pretend snowflakes flutter down onto them. She wondered if it was strange that she had never played in snow or built a snowman.

'Come along, Nancy,' called her mother from a shop doorway. 'I have a lot to do.'

Nancy sighed, 'You have a lot to do,' she muttered to herself. 'What about me? I never have anything to do.' She followed her mother.

Inside the store, Veronica held various dresses and fluffy jumpers against Nancy, squinting at each one, pulling shoulders straight and checking hem lengths. She draped item after item over her left arm, expertly rifling through racks with her right hand, all the time holding her handbag and shopping bags, and dragging Nancy along beside her. Nancy thought that clothes shopping was a skill that only mothers were expert at, and she doubted she would ever grow up to master it.

As they headed for the till, a tall thin woman stepped out from behind a mannequin and blocked their way.

'Mrs Bloom!' the woman gushed. 'How lovely to see you! How are you?'

Nancy saw her mother pause ever so briefly, then placed a bright smile on her face.

'Hello, Mrs Trott. Things are good with us, thank you. How are you and the family?'

'Oh, same old, same old.' Mrs Trott dismissed her family's wellbeing with a flap of her hand and focussed her gleaming smile firmly on Mrs Bloom. 'Now, I've been thinking about the Christmas fete and I have some wonderful ideas for you. We must get together and discuss it.'

'Absolutely,' said Mrs Bloom. 'I'll give you a call.'

She started to walk to the cash register, but Mrs Trott stopped her, pulling a large leather diary from her bag. 'Well, why don't we make a date now,' she beamed. 'We can always change it later.'

Mrs Bloom paused. 'I'll have to check my diary,' she said, politely. 'I'm a little busy right now shopping for my daughter.'

Mrs Trott seemed to noticed Nancy for the first time. 'Oh, of course. I won't keep you. She turned her shiny teeth to Nancy. 'And how are you, little Alice?'

'Erm…fine, thank you,' said Nancy, confused.

A look of horror crossed Mrs Trott's face. She looked at Mrs Bloom. 'I mean….I'm sorry….I meant….Nancy, isn't it?'

There was an uncomfortable moment of confusion as the shocked face of Mrs Trott moved from Nancy to her mother.

Mrs Bloom had a forced smile on her own face. 'I'll call you, Miranda,' she said firmly through gritted teeth.

'Yes!' Mrs Miranda Trott stuffed the diary back into her bag. 'I must be going. Goodbye. Goodbye……Nancy.'

She rushed away backwards, almost crashing into the nearby mannequin, then walking away quickly with a brief backward glance.

'What was that about?' Nancy asked her mother, baffled.

Veronica shook her head. 'That woman!' She checked the items on her arm. 'Come one, let's pay for these,' and headed off to the tills.

Nancy followed, bewildered.

Chapter Three

After church on Sunday, Mayor Bloom invited several Very Important Business People back to the Manor for lunch.

Nancy was brought into the drawing room before lunch to be paraded and introduced. She smiled sweetly in her best Sunday dress. Everyone smiled back.

Nancy always wondered what Very Important Business People actually did all day. She imagined them arriving in warm leathery offices once everyone was already doing work, sitting in front of shiny black desks, drinking coffee, smiling at computer screens and big diaries and complimenting themselves on being VIBPs (Very Important Business People). She thought they had lunch in busy expensive restaurants (two hours, because one wouldn't be long enough), drinking red wine, napping in their offices between long chatty phone calls with other VIBPs. Then going home to crackling fires and port.

She wondered if being a VIBP was a real career choice, because it sounded like a good one to her.

Mayor Bloom was unveiling his big plans for the Christmas Competition. For this, the village needed funding. It didn't seem to strike him as ironic to spend tens of thousands of pounds in order to win tens of thousands of pounds. For the village it was all about the winning. Sunny Meadows residents were wealthy and successful, and they just wanted everyone else to know about it.

Only the adults were lunching together, so Nancy was eating in the kitchen with Millie.

'They talk about such boring things,' she complained to her tutor, as the dining room door swung open to let the hired caterer serve the diners.

'We still need to get around the problem of the boundary line,' boomed a blustery voice. 'We can't have half our Winter Wonderland spilling over into Hogweed Fields…'

Millie put down plates and drinks and sat down. Nancy liked her. She was young and kind and had longish bright orange hair that was kind of crinkly.

'It probably isn't boring to them,' said Millie. 'Maybe they think you're boring.'

Nancy shrugged. 'Probably.' She ate her peanut butter and jam sandwich. The others were having lamb and mint sauce and new potatoes, but Millie let her eat things she liked. 'Maybe I am boring.'

'Do you have homework left to do?'

'It's *Sunday*. Anyway, I already did it.'

'You're a good girl, Nancy.'

'Yeah, I know.' She looked at Millie closely. 'Can I ask you a question?'

'Okay.'

'What is school like?'

Millie thought for a moment. 'Well, they are all different. Mostly, they are busy and loud, and people fight. Why?'

'I've just been wondering. I'd have more friends if I went to school.'

'You have friends.' Millie reached across and picked up Nancy's pigtail. 'You're a good girl,' she said again, stroking the girl's hair with her thumb. 'Everyone likes you.' She scrunched up her nose. 'Are you okay?' she said, quietly.

Nancy shrugged again.

'Tell you what,' said Millie. 'After your studies tomorrow, why don't we have Carrie-Ann and Marguerite round for tea? That will cheer you up.'

'Thanks.' Nancy thought that was the last thing she needed.

When Carrie-Ann and Marguerite arrived the next afternoon, Mrs Bloom invited their mothers to stay for coffee. The girls escaped to the garden in the late-Autumn sunshine and had their afternoon tea on the patio.

Carrie-Ann was similar to Millie in colouring, except her red hair was poker straight. Marguerite was an ice blonde, and exceptionally pretty.

After cake and forced social niceties, Nancy suggested playing on the swings, but the others declined.

'I just had my nails done,' said Carrie-Ann. 'Do you like?' She waved her fingers in Nancy's face. Bright pink claws waggled on the end of them. They seemed pretty pointless and impractical.

'Nice,' said Nancy.

After a while, Nancy went to play on the swings on her own, leaving the other girls to a long, dull conversation about hair extensions.

Her mother would be annoyed with her for being a bad hostess, but there was only so much banality she could take.

'Come and play,' she called. 'You're being boring.'

'Don't be so rude!' snapped Marguerite.

'Rude is ignoring someone after you've come their house,' pointed out Nancy.

'It isn't even your house,' said Carrie-Ann. 'You only live here because of your dad's job. When he stops being Mayor, you'll probably end up in a shack somewhere.' Marguerite laughed loudly.

'Take that back!' said Nancy, jumping off her swing. She picked up a clot of earth and threw it at the table in anger. Quite unintentionally, she hit Carrie-Ann right in the middle of her perfectly made up face.

'How dare you!' Carrie-Ann leapt off her chair, marched over to Nancy and slapped her hard across the face. Marguerite screamed, bringing the mothers outside.

The bright red mark across Nancy's cheek made a good case for her innocence, and after being scolded firmly by her mother, Carrie-Ann was sent upstairs to wash up, accompanied by the crying Marguerite.

Nancy stayed outside to calm down. She felt bad for her angry reaction. What Carrie-Ann had said was probably true. She decided to go inside and explain to the parents that it was her fault.

The door to the drawing room was ajar, and as she approached, she heard her mother's voice.

'It is unacceptable behaviour, Marilyn. You must see that.'

'I know, I know. I just don't know where we are going wrong with her.'

'You've given her everything,' said sultry French accent of Marguerite's mother. 'You have done so much. You can't blame yourself for a bad one.'

'Thankyou, Francine. It's difficult, but she's our only one.'

'You could try again.' Nancy saw Francine take a sip from her china teacup and replace it elegantly on the saucer in her hand. 'I'm sure no-one would hold this against you.'

'I'm sorry Marilyn,' said Veronica, firmly,' but it seems quite clear that Carrie-Ann isn't working out.'

'Oh, no,' said Carrie-Ann's mother. 'There's still time…'

'I'm sorry, but I'm sure everyone else will agree. It may be time to dissimilate.'

'No, please…' Carrie-Ann's mother began to sob.

Francine patted the crying woman's shoulder. 'Now, now,' she said, coolly. 'It's not the end of the world.'

'We can't risk any negative impacts on our own children,' said Veronica. 'We'll discuss it with the others tomorrow, but I'm sure I know what the outcome will be.'

Nancy stood behind the door, wide-eyed, feeling like she had just witnessed something very dangerous.

She crept away and ran upstairs to find the other girls. It seemed a good idea to keep them out of the way for a while.

After a beautifully warm start to November, the weather changed suddenly one morning.

Nancy woke up to frost on her window and a cold draft through her room. She was glad of it. She was a winter girl. Even as her child, her favourite book had been the Snow Queen.

She breathed her warm breath on the windowpane and wrote 'HI' with her finger in the condensation.

Her father knocked on her bedroom door, and entered.

'Good morning, missy! Do you fancy skiving off your studies for the morning and coming out with your old dad? I'll buy you a hot chocolate?'

'I'd love to!'

'Good! Meet you in the car at 9.'

For once, she was glad that her mother had bundled her up in too many fluffy clothes. Even the back of the car was chilly until the heater kicked in.

The Mayor had invited two others along, his solicitor Martin and his secretary Nadine. Nancy knew them both well, so she didn't mind. Nadine sat in the back with her and gave her paper to draw on.

They drove to the outskirts of the village, where Appleseed Farm had its land. It was a lovely area in the fresh dewy morning light. The four visitors left the car and walked into the fields.

'Are we allowed to be here?' Nancy asked her father, looking around for an angry farmer with an air rifle.

'Not to worry,' said Mayor Bloom. 'We're perfectly legal. Eh, Martin?'

The solicitor agreed. 'We have Monty's full permission to use the land until January.'

The field stretched out flat and green, ending in a clump of trees and buildings at the far end.

Mayor Bloom put his arm around Nancy's shoulder.

'Look at all this,' he said. 'In a few week's time, this will be the heart of our Christmas contest. We're going to build our very own Winter Wonderland, Santa's grotto and reindeer stables. We'll be the talk of the country.'

Nancy looked doubtfully at the blank space. 'Won't that take time?'

'Yes! Time, money, dedication! Luckily, we have a wonderful team on our side.' He kissed the top of Nancy's head. 'You may not see much of me for a few weeks, but it'll be worth it.'

The adults walked around for a while, studying large plans and taking photos.

Martin indicated the group of buildings on the horizon. 'There's your problem. Franklin's Garage'.

'Ah, yes,' said the Mayor. 'I know of it. I used to know it well.'

'They blocked permission for the build on the grounds that it would ruin business. Unknown to them, the business lies almost entirely over the boundary line onto the farmland. They pay all their bills and taxes in Hogweed Fields, but technically, they are trespassing in Sunny Meadows.'

'I see,' said the Mayor. 'Then maybe they need a little lesson in playing nice. Eh, Nancy?' He winked and chuckled. 'Come on, girl, I owe you a hot chocolate.'

Nancy felt troubled. She didn't like the idea of her father and his cronies bullying someone who had less than them. Less money, less power, less land, less hope.

She saw a couple of children drop down from the trees and run laughing over the boundary line. *They should be at school*, she thought to herself.

But, then again, so should she.

Chapter Four

There is the old saying, 'Charity begins at home.' For Nancy's father, the same went for Christmas.

The day after Bonfire Night, there was a lot of commotion downstairs and unfamiliar voices floating up through the open bedroom window.

Nancy looked outside to see a large moving van on the lawn, and a lone giant plastic reindeer wrapped in bubble wrap.

She sighed. 'And so it begins.'

She went downstairs in her pyjamas, stopping at the bottom of the stairs to let two strange men pass by carrying a long package in a styrofoam box.

'Morning,' said one of the men, struggling with his end. They manoeuvred it through a narrow doorway towards the dining room.

Nancy wandered around, looking for her parents.

'Hi, Nancy,' said a complete stranger in the kitchen. 'Would you like some coffee?'

'I don't drink coffee,' said Nancy. 'I'm ten.'

She went from room to room, encountering packages and people at every turn. Eventually she found her father in the garden, beside the plastic reindeer.

'I wish it was a real one,' said her father, wistfully. 'Isn't he a beauty?'

To Nancy, it looked a bit squashed, and its eyes seemed to point in different directions.

'It's alright,' she admitted. 'What's going on?'

'Christmas decorations!'

'It's the 6th of November.'

'Exactly! We're 6 days behind. So I called in reinforcements.' He put his arm round Nancy and led her back into the house. 'We have to lead the way, and the whole village will follow. That's how we'll win.'

Nadine was in the conservatory draped in streams of fairy lights. 'I have no idea what I'm doing!' she panicked.

Mayor Bloom pointed Nancy in the direction of the kitchen. 'I have to help here. Go and find someone to make you some breakfast. Just ask. They're all employees, so they'll do whatever you say.'

Nancy went to the kitchen. She got a piece of bread, smeared butter and berry jam on it, and went looking for her mother.

She found her on the phone in the hallway.

'Mum, what am I doing today?' she asked.

Veronica covered the mouthpiece with her hand.

'Not now, Nancy. Be a good girl and go and get dressed.'

'What shall I wear?'

'Anything.'

Nancy took her piece of bread back to her bedroom and looked through the clothes in her dressing room.

'Anything, eh?'

She settled on stripey woollen tights, a frilly party dress, and a wooly hat with a bear on it.

Outside the window, a voice called, 'Blitzen only has three legs. Can we get away with that or does it have to go back?'

Nancy lay on her bed, bored. She was getting tired of being a good girl. She wondered what would happen if she ran away from home, and how long it would take for everyone to notice.

They might not even miss her until New Year. Maybe not even then.

She imagined her parents sitting around in their twilight years, white-haired and wrinkled, and one of them saying suddenly, 'Wait! Didn't we used to have a child?'

She picked up a notepad and pen, and doodled for a while, then wrote:

'There was a little girl, who had a little world,
Filled with cruelty and malice.
When she was good, she was very, very good,
And when she was bad, she was Alice.'

That evening, Nancy sat with her mother in front of a roaring fire, putting cards in envelopes. The Mayor had decided that in the spirit of leading the way, they should send a card to everyone in the village.

Nancy personally thought that he was starting to get a bit carried away with it all.

A silver fairy hung in one of the drawing room windows, framed by the frost outside. Nancy had named her Fay. She would have liked a sister called Fay. Fairy lights reflected in Fay, making her glitter with colour as she turned in the draft.

Her mother was in a big squashy armchair, crocheting.

'Mum,' she said. 'Who's Alice?'

'I have no idea,' said her mother, not looking up.

'Mrs Trott called me Alice.'

'Well, Mrs Trott's been calling me Valerie for three years. I have no idea who Valerie is, either.'

'Mum,' she said. 'Do you think I could go to school one day?'

'I doubt it. You wouldn't like it.'

'Well, could I try at least?'

'What's the point? You'll only be unhappy.'
'Is there another way I could make some friends?'
'You have friends.'
'Not really.' She paused. 'I haven't seen Carrie-Ann for over a week.'
'I think she might be on on holiday. I haven't heard from Francine for a few days.'
'I don't much like Carrie-Ann.'
'You mustn't say mean things, Nancy. You're better than that.'
'Mum, do you love me?'
Veronica stopped knitting and looked up. 'Well, what kind of thing is that to ask? And what's with the twenty questions, anyway? Are you bored? Maybe you should go and get a snack.'
'My fingers do hurt,' said Nancy, pushing aside the envelopes.
In the kitchen, Millicent was rolling out pastry on the marble kitchen island. Nancy sat on a high stool next to her.
'Millie, do you think my mum loves me?'
'Of course she does. Here.' She gave Nancy some off-cuts off pastry to play with. Nancy liked the squishy feel of it between her fingers. She started to make shapes from it.
'Millie, what is your job?'
Millicent laughed. 'Well, if you don't know the answer to that by now, we've wasted a lot of time on your studies! What do you think I am, the gardener?'
Nancy shrugged. 'You garden sometimes.'
'I do a lot of things sometimes.'
'Like what?'
'Like make jam tarts. What flavour do you want?'

'Strawberry. And maybe some blackcurrant.' She thought, building a little pastry man. 'Millie, where will you go when you leave here?'

'Am I leaving?'

'Are you?'

'Not that I know of.' She started to cut out pastry shapes with cookie cutters - Santa, reindeers, trees.

'If you were, where would you go? Do you have family?'

'Not really. I had a sister, but she died.'

'What was her name?'

'Jennifer.'

'How did she die?'

'She was very ill.'

'Was it nice, having a sister?'

'Yes, it was. Now, why all the questions? What's on your mind?'

'Nothing.' Nancy let out a deep sigh and put a dollop of strawberry jam on her flat pastry man. 'Can I cook him?'

'Tell you what, you be in charge of jam, and then we'll cook them all. Deal?

Nancy smiled. 'Deal.' She decided to pretend that Millie was her sister and that she was Jennifer, still alive. That would have been nice.

Her sister gave her gleaming teaspoons and jars and they set to work.

Chapter Five

As well as being the Mayor's wife, a good parishioner, and a fine upstanding member of the local community, Veronica Bloom was also 'very big' in the WI. - the Wives Institute. In fact, she was the president of the local chapter.

Every two weeks or so, the village ladies met in one place or another to talk, drink tea (or wine on special occasions), listen to inspirational speakers, learn different crafts or skills, and bake for various fundraisers and charity sales.

For several months now, the ladies had been meeting fortnightly at the Manor to learn to crochet in preparation for a charity jumble sale. What began as nervous first tries for some soon resulted in scarfs, hats, mittens, cardigans and blankets pouring out of the needles and filling the spare room.

The jumble sale took place one drizzly Saturday afternoon in the dark church hall. Everyone who came in was damp and shaking out umbrellas, and as their coats dried out in the central heating, the hall soon began to take on the musty smell of wet dogs.

As always with her mother's activities, Nancy was roped in to help. She stood behind a stall piled high with coloured woollen items. She tried on a bright red crocheted hat with a bright blue crocheted flower on the side. It was different, but she kind of liked it.

'Nancy, take that off!' hissed her mother. 'You look ridiculous'.

'I see you are admiring one of my hats,' said Mrs Blatch, appearing at the table. 'I'm rather proud of that one.'

'Oh, it's lovely,' said Mrs Bloom, straightening the hat and smoothing Nancy's hair. 'We were just saying how pretty it is.'

'Well, if you want it, you'd better buy it before someone snaps it up.' Mrs Blatch drifted away to the next table.

'Take it off!' hissed Veronica.

Nancy put the hat on a pile of others just like it.

'Can I go and get a cake?' she asked.

'Okay. But don't be too long. It's getting busy.'

Nancy didn't think a bunch of old ladies and a few stray children really counted as busy, but she didn't waste time in heading straight for the bake stall. Francine and Marguerite sat guarding plates of cakes, breads, scones and jars of homemade jam.

'Could I have a cupcake please?' she asked Francine. She chose a chocolate one with pink icing and handed over her money.

'Hi Marguerite. You look nice.' She certainly did, with her blonde hair in ringlets like a china doll.

'Thanks. So do you. I made those pink ones.'

Nancy tried her cake. 'It's delicious.'

'Where is your father today?' asked Francine. 'I thought he would have been here to keep an eye on us.'

'He's coming later. They started construction on the Winter Wonderland, and he had to be there for press photos.'

'How nice for him,' purred Francine. She turned away, snootily.

Nancy was confused. She used to think Francine was nice, but now she was getting a bad feeling about her.

'I'll speak to you later,' whispered Marguerite behind her hand, glancing at her mother's turned back.

'See you later,' said Nancy, loudly.

She wondered from stall to stall, ignoring her mother's attempts to get her attention from across the room. She could make her help at these things, but she couldn't make her enjoy it.

At the book stall, she saw Marilyn Foster sorting titles into alphabetical order.

'Hi,' said Nancy.

Marilyn started with a shock and held a hand to her heart. She looked up.

'I'm so sorry, Nancy. You scared me.'

'Sorry.' She ate her cake and pretended to browse through the books. Lots of local books, lots of old fusty classics.

'Where is Carrie-Ann?' Nancy asked, casually. 'I haven't seen her.'

'Oh, she's…ill.' Marilyn busied herself with boxes of books behind the counter.

'I'm sorry to hear that. Perhaps I could stop by and try to cheer her up.'

'Oh, I'm sorry. She's infectious. She isn't allowed visitors.'

'I'll call her then, shall I?'

'I'm not sure I…'

Marilyn looked relieved as Veronica interrupted.

'Nancy, you've been ages. Go back to the table. I have things to do.'

'Of course, mother.' She stared at Mrs Foster. 'You should try a cake,' she said, brightly. 'They are really good.'

'I….I will.'

Nancy went back to the heaps of brightly coloured wool, but her mind was dark and troubled.

Horatio Bloom always entered the room as though he was a celebrity. His size, his majestic moustaches and his booming voice meant that he was impossible to ignore.

Nancy was relieved when he arrived, but as always, he was flocked within seconds, and she had to wait her turn to speak to him.

She didn't mind. She was proud of her dad. He worked hard. She just wished he spent as much time with his own family as he did with other peoples'.

Eventually, after admiring candles, trying cakes, complimenting lemonade, and losing three goes on the tombola, he made his way round to her table.

'How's my girl?' he smiled.

'Fine,' said Nancy. 'Bored.'

'You're doing a good job. Your mother tells me you've sold quite a lot.'

'Not really.'

'Well, every penny counts. And we need all we can get. There's talk of getting in some real live reindeers.'

'Aren't they endangered or something?'

'Who knows? That's Martin's problem.' He picked up a yellow scarf and held it against him. 'What do you think?'

Nancy giggled. 'Very pretty.'

'I'll tell you what,' said her father, pulling a handful of coins from his pocket. 'I'll make a donation, but you can keep the scarf. I'm not sure it's quite my colour.'

Nancy put the money in the tin.

'Now, I'd better go and mingle before your mother stares at me for much longer. She needs someone to announce the winner of the silent raffle, or some such nonsense.' He lowered his voice. 'I do hope it isn't that awful Mrs Mouse. She always tries to kiss me.' He headed off toward his wife, but was stopped on the way. 'Mrs Mouse, how lovely to see you…'

Marguerite caught Nancy outside the toilets and pulled her inside.
'Nancy, I'm scared,' she whispered.
'Of what?'
'I don't know. I think something is wrong with Carrie-Ann.'
'She's ill.'
'No, that isn't true. I went to her house and spoke to her dad. He said she went to visit an aunt and he didn't know when she would be back.'
'But her mum just told me she's infectious.'
'It's a lie. I think she's missing.'
'But wouldn't her mother know about that?'
'I think she does.'
'What do you mean?'
'Something strange is going on. I heard…'
A toilet flushed in one of the cubicles, and Nancy grabbed Marguerite's hand and dragged her outside and round a corner. They heard sounds of someone washing their hands, then the door opening.
Nancy peered round the corner to see Francine leaving the bathroom, her face expressionless, but her eyes dark.

Chapter Six

One dreary afternoon, when her parents were out and Millie was preparing dinner, Nancy pulled on boots and a hoody and slipped out the french doors into the garden.

The Manor gardens were large, and much of it was overgrown, although soon to be cleared up by landscapers. In fact, a mini-digger and a wood chipper sat idly on the grass, waiting for Monday morning workers.

Nancy picked up her scooter and scooted along the path that ran the length of the long garden, and round a corner by the sheds.

The sheds were black wood and closely grouped together. They were very ugly, but her father hadn't got round to doing anything with them yet. When the home comes with the job, it is important to be careful how much money is spent on something that you may not be around long enough to enjoy.

One of the sheds had been cleared out, though, with stacks of logs, old kitchen cabinets and a rusty wheelbarrow parked inside. The door was locked, but through the grimy window, Nancy saw lots of new white poles and cases of something. She worried that her father had some kind of embarrassing festive extravaganza planned that she would be dragged into.

For a moment, she thought there was a reflection behind her in the glass.

It was unmistakably the reflection of a small boy, watching her from the trees, but he vanished as quickly as she noticed him.

There were lots of dark trees and bramble bushes, far too thick to walk through. Of to the left, though, was a narrow gap just wide enough for a little girl. Leaning her scooter against the shed, she squeezed herself through the gap, and found a thin worn path behind it.

My mother would kill me if she saw me doing this, she thought, and the idea gave her a nice sense of rebelliousness. *I was just exploring in the garden*, she practised, *seeing if I could get any ideas to help daddy.*

She was hoping that the trees would come out somewhere soon, but she seemed to be going deeper and deeper into the woods.

Am I still in the garden? she wondered.

A few moments later, there was a very climbable tree, with wide pale branches and good footholds. Nancy hoisted herself up through its leaves until she she found a flat branch to sit on. Hugging onto the trunk, she looked around. The views were lovely from up here, looking down into the valley of the village with its pretty little streets drifting away to a misty, rainy horizon. On a clear day, she would be able to see for miles around.

It was immediately apparent that she was still in the garden, but had veered far round to the left away from the main road. Beyond the woods was a long field, and a small figure of a boy was running away across it, in the direction of Hogweed Fields.

Behind her, she heard her mother's voice from the direction of the house. Quickly, she slid down the tree and ran back to the garden.

Dinner that evening was a rare family affair. Nancy helped herself to chicken and gravy from a large ceramic casserole on the table. She didn't like chicken much, but she was hungry.

She had been scolded for arriving at the back door dirty and covered in leaves, until she claimed to have fallen and then cried for a while. Her mother put her in a hot bubble bath and allowed her to spend the afternoon in her pyjamas.

Mayor Bloom put a few roast potatoes on Nancy's plate, knowing full well she would never eat them. He always had an attitude of 'take them anyway so your plate looks full', which seemed pretty pointless. It was the same with sprouts on Christmas day.

'How is the build coming on, Horatio?' asked Mrs Bloom. She looked very elegant this particular evening. She was trying her hair in a new upsweep style, and it suited her slim frame and long neck.

The Mayor dabbed his moustache with a white linen napkin. 'Wonderful! Wonderful! Coming along fine. Apart from the…..er…..trouble.'

'What trouble?' asked Nancy.

'Nothing much. Just a little legal trouble. Some business slowing things down a bit. Not to worry. All is well, little one.' He ruffled Nancy's damp hair.

'Well, I have wonderful news,' said Veronica. 'I was speaking to Mary Moore this afternoon. The school is holding a Nativity play in their new hall, and has promised to put all proceeds towards the contest bid. '

'Oh, that is wonderful news,' said her father. 'Those excellent children.'

'Can we go?' asked Nancy, quickly.

'It depends when it is,' said her mother.

'But we should go. They are giving away money they could use themselves. Daddy said we have to lead the way.'

'And so we do.' Mayor Bloom took a celebratory swig of red wine. He was a man truly satisfied with his life, a man with a purpose.

Mrs Bloom sipped her white wine and patted her hair to make sure it was still in place.

Nancy sensed a positive mood in the air, and hazarded another question.
'Mum, can I have a pet?'
'What kind of pet?'
'A dog?'
'No.'
'A mouse?'
'Maybe. Eat your casserole like a good girl.'
Nancy thought about a mouse. She would call it Jerry.

A whirl of activities started to take over, as though her parents were working very hard to keep her busy.
Church services, charity events, music lessons, theatre trips, all combined with following her mother to voluntary evenings in aid of the Christmas plans.
There wasn't any opportunity to explore the gardens or the woods any further. She had asked Millicent where the fields led to, but Millicent wasn't sure.
Nancy looked out of the upstairs windows and hoped to see a shadowy figure at the end of the path, but there was only ever her own reflection looking back.
Work on the village and the Winter Wonderland continued throughout November. The villages would be judged on 23rd December, and the winners announced that evening right there in Sunny Meadows, which was the previous year's winner.
So sure were the villagers on winning that a celebration party was already being planned, to be shared between the gracious winners and the disappointed losers.
The village was looking very pretty in the Autumn light. All shops, salons and public houses were getting

into the swing of things, with decorations popping up nice and early all over the place.

A couple of shops decided to take on themes for their window fronts and displays. One went for the full Victorian style 'A Christmas Carol theme', with fake frost on the windows, boxes of chocolates and violet creams, and a big fake turkey wrapped up with red ribbon.

Nancy spent a long time staring in the window, taking in the authentic scene, and imagining she was The Little Match Girl, hungry and cold on Christmas Eve.

She imagined that she was really a poor orphan and had been taken in by a rich family and named Nancy Bloom. She imagined her real name was Lucy Miller and that she had lots of poor brothers and sisters out there in the world looking for her. One day she would find them and bring them to live with her at The Manor and they would be so grateful and proud of her for saving them.

Fairy lights were strung through the trees down the High Street and The Avenue. Nancy made sure to dawdle every time her parents took her out to the shops, so that she could be there at 4 when the light began to fade and the lights went on. They lit up everything like strings of diamonds and rubies glittering in the dark branches.

Chapter Seven

The evening of the Nativity came around on a crisp, chilly December day.

Nancy felt a certain excitement as she got ready in her room. She wore a pretty red dress and put her hair in two long plaits. So much of her life was spent around adults that she could hardly wait to be around other children, and to actually see inside the school.

It was strange to her that other children dreaded school, and hated hours and hours stuck in a room together. It was something she'd always dreamed of. She even longed to wear a uniform every day. It must be nice to know what you were wearing every day, rather than wake up to find your mother had chosen sparkly leggings and an itchy white sweater that was too big and hot, just because she thought it suited your colouring.

Veronica thoroughly enjoyed having a pretty daughter, and she liked to show her off. She seemed to take it as another extension of her own successes, rather than just random and haphazard genetics.

But tonight, Nancy was happy to dress well for her parents, because she was so happy that they were taking her to the concert at all.

As they pulled in to the school car park, Nancy began to get nervous, which was ridiculous, because it wasn't going to be her up there on the stage. The building was all lit up, so many rooms, and the car park was full already.

She got nervous sometimes because her family was quite well known in the village, and people treated them differently. A lot of people would enjoy having the special attention, but Nancy found it quite embarrassing.

She knew everyone would be looking at them and judging them. She knew that she looked like a pretty little rich girl, and she didn't like that at all.

Her fears were well-founded. As they entered the brightly-lit hall and walked down the centre aisle between the crowded seats, everyone turned to look at them. Nancy followed timidly in her wake of her parents, smiling at the children she saw.

Some children smiled back, but others scowled quite meanly, and thought Nancy, quite unnecessarily. She didn't even know them. They didn't know that she really was sweet and wanted to be their friend.

There were seats saved for them right at the front row. Again, this bothered her. They didn't do anything to deserve those seats. She wished they could swap with the people in the back row.

Veronica placed Nancy between herself and Mayor Bloom. Nancy was grateful for that. She didn't want to sit next to a stranger all evening.

The concert was good fun. Her parents were in good moods. Her father especially loved every moment, and laughed heartily in all the right places. The children beamed with pleasure at the front row and seemed to be fuelled by his enjoyment. They sang louder, danced better, and directed all the funny lines straight to him.

Nancy thought it would be wonderful to be up there on the stage. She imagined being able to go to school next year and being popular and loved. She imagined auditioning for a small role in the Christmas play, maybe as a sheep, and the teacher saying, 'This girl is wonderful. She must have the lead role', and she playing Mary to a packed auditorium, receiving a standing ovation, and being discovered by a Hollywood film company. This time next year she could be a huge star, letting her parents visit on special occasions, but doing whatever she wanted the rest of the time.

After the concert, Mayor and Mrs Bloom got caught up with various members of the community wanting to speak to them. They assumed Nancy was right beside them, as she knew she was supposed to be, but Nancy took the opportunity to step ever so slightly away. Just a few steps, but it felt very freeing.

I'm in school and there are other children, and some of them might want to be my friends, she thought.

She put a friendly and approachable look on her face, and hoped to hook one in. It worked.

'Hi,' said a young blonde girl. 'You're Nancy Bloom, aren't you?'

'Hi,' said Nancy, quietly, trying to hide her nerves and gratitude. 'I mean, yes.'

'I'm Kitty,' said the girl. 'How come we never see you at school?'

'I'm not allowed to go to school. I have a tutor.'

'God, you're so lucky.'

'I guess so.'

'Do you want to come over and meet my friends?'

'Yeah, I'd love to.'

Unfortunately, Veronica turned just as she was about to walk away.

How does she always know, like she has a radar?

'Time to go, Nancy. Come and get your coat.'

Nancy ever so briefly thought of ignoring her mother and going with Kitty anyway. She looked from one to the other.

'Sorry,' she said to Kitty. 'I have to go.'

Kitty shrugged and went back to her friends, leaving Nancy with a sick feeling in her stomach.

'Nancy!'

'Yes, mother.'

A journalist from the local paper snapped their photo, the three Blooms smiling together in black and white.

Chapter Eight

The Wives Institute didn't meet in private very often.

Usually they held open coffee mornings, or met in each other's houses when their families were also present. Sometimes they held events in the town hall or in other public places. Once they even met in a pub, although that wasn't necessarily their style, and Mrs Mouse had got a little bit carried away and got a bit too tipsy on sherry.

On December 9th, a very important message was sent to each member to meet in their most secret meeting place. This was something that very rarely happened, and indicated that it was a very important situation. Refusing to attend was not an option.

Eight wooden chairs were set in a circle in the church basement, which was lit only by candlelight. It was a dank, spooky, bare room, and a dreary place to hold any kind of get-together.

'Is this lighting really necessary?' asked Veronica Bloom. 'It seems a little melodramatic.'

'Just trying to set the mood,' said Mrs Harriet, seated to her left. 'This is serious business, and some people seem to be forgetting that. Speak of the devil,' as Mrs Blatch burst through the door ten minutes late.

'So sorry,' said Mrs Blatch. 'I couldn't find anyone to watch Maggie for me. Her dad got called in to work at the last minute.'

'That isn't our problem,' said Francine La Mer, coldly. 'We have bigger issues here, and we have been waiting to start.'

Mrs Blatch put down her handbag and her hat and sunk into the only empty chair.

'Shall we begin?' said Mrs Bloom. Everyone nodded. 'I thought we should get together to discuss our progress. Obviously, some of us are doing better than others...'

Everyone looked at Marilyn Foster, who looked down at her shoes.

'Don't worry, Marilyn,' said Mrs Harriet. 'There's still hope. You're not out yet.'

'Almost, though,' smirked Mrs La Mer.

'Yes, yes,' said Mrs Bloom. 'We all agree that what happened with Carrie-Ann was very unfortunate. But nothing is concluded yet. We still have a long way to go.'

'I think the main concern to us right now is that people are starting to ask questions,' said Mrs Harriet to the group. 'We have worked too long and too hard to let everything begin to unravel now.'

'Nothing is unravelling,' said Mrs Bloom, 'and there is no way anyone can do us real harm. After all, we are still in control.'

'Most of us,' said Francine, cattily.

'Meaning what exactly, Francine?'

'Meaning have you looked at your own household, Veronica?'

There was a shocked silence, and several loud intakes of breath.

'I can't imagine what you are implying,' said Mrs Bloom, 'but I must warn you that there is a hierarchy in this room, and insolence will not be tolerated.'

The atmosphere in the cold damp cellar became even more stifling, and the temperature seemed to dip several degrees.

'Veronica,' said Mrs Blatch. 'While our original intentions here were good ones, and we have provided children to many who couldn't have them, I feel we may be losing sight of our aims. When we first came to this place, it was to live among the natives, to learn their ways, to observe them. I think we may be wielding our power unfairly.'

'Oh shush,' said Mrs La Mer. 'You were as much a part of this as anyone, Mrs Blatch. We live with these beings, we bake cakes, we knit, blah blah blah. It is dull and monotonous. So we make children, we find entertainment, we play games. Some watch TV, we watch the world, we watch life.'

'I think we have done a little more than that,' snapped Veronica.

'If I may interrupt,' said the timid Mrs Twigg. She blushed as the ladies looked her way, except for Veronica and Francine, who were glaring icily at each other. 'I can't imagine,' continued Mrs Twig, quietly, 'that anyone could have a word to say against the Bloom family. The Mayor has transformed this town and created the ideal community for our experiment.'

'I don't think it's the Mayor that Mrs La Mer is speaking of,' said Carrie-Ann's mother, slowly. 'Is it?'

Mrs Bloom turned her attention to Marilyn Foster, who shrunk under her gaze, wishing she hadn't spoken.

The group sat silently for a moment. there was a stand-off ensuing, and no-one wanted to get caught in the cross-fire.

'Are you speaking about my daughter?' said Veronica. Her attitude was one of a lioness sensing danger for her young.

'Your daughter Nancy is asking a lot of questions,' said Francine La Mer. 'I am sensing some rebelliousness in her, and she is trying to rub that rebelliousness off on my Marguerite.'

'Oh, no,' said Mrs Blatch. 'Nancy is a wonderful girl. She is a perfect example of how our children should be.'

'Do you have any proof?' said Mrs Bloom to Francine.

'I have an investment here, Veronica, and no-one is beyond criticism, are they not? Or was this an unfair game right from the start?'

'Oh, don't call it a game,' said Mrs Mouse. 'It has become bigger than that. We have grown to love our children.'

'I loved Carrie-Ann,' said Mrs Foster.

'Well, then you should have controlled her better,' snapped Veronica. 'Her temper would always be her undoing, and the fault for that lies entirely at your feet.'

'And so the responsibility for Nancy lies at yours, Veronica,' said Francine.

'I'm sorry, Veronica,' said Mrs Harriet, 'but I have to agree with Francine. There can be no favouritism here. No-one is above reproach. You may have to be on your last chance with her, just as Marilyn was at our last meeting.'

'Shall we vote?' said Francine. 'Motion to issue a final warning?'

The women, except for Veronica, raised their right hands.

Mrs Mouse seemed upset. 'Poor Nancy. She's such a good one.'

'Motion granted,' said Francine, licking her lips like the cat that got the cream. 'I'm sorry, Veronica, but it seems dissimilation may be inevitable.'

That night, Veronica Bloom crept into the house while everyone was sleeping.

She looked into her bedroom. In the bed Mayor Bloom lay snoring like a camel. His rhythmic snorting and purring noises shook the room.

Veronica pulled the bedroom door closed, quietly, and went across the hall.

Nancy was sleeping in her big soft bed, her long hair fanned out behind her on the white pillow. A soft blue dog was gripped in her left arm. On the bedside table were a book and a glass of water. She had been reading before bed, just like she was supposed to.

She really was such a very good daughter.

Veronica felt a huge wave of emotion for the child. It was a feeling she was unaccustomed to.

In the darkness, she reached out her hand and stroked the girl's hair fondly.

It really would be a great shame to have to let her go.

Part Two - Alice

Chapter Nine

A cold, heavy November rain fell down on Alice, washing the dirt from her face and hands. Her hair stuck to her face in wet splatters, and her thin clothes clung to her.

She trudged through the empty streets, not rushing, quietly making her way home. There was nothing to rush for. She was drenched, but would soon be dry.

A little wet terrier ran past her, heading the other way. Alice hoped he had somewhere warm to go.

She eventually arrived home, and let herself into the house. There was no-one home yet. Alice peeled off her wet clothes onto her bedroom floor and got into a hot shower.

She was dry and in warm clothes when her parents arrived home, one after the other, from work.

Alice had already put a pot of tea, crusty bread, bright yellow butter, and large cups on the wooden kitchen table. She had chunks of cheese, cold deli meats and boiled eggs ready in the fridge and the saucepan.

She was sitting in the chair nearest the stove to dry her damp hair.

Alice's mother, Martha, arrived first, dishevelled and harassed, throwing her wet coat and bag on a chair by the door.

'Have you done your homework?' she said to Alice, by way of greeting.

'Yes,' lied Alice.

The banging of the front door signified the arrival of her father, and Alice brightened.

'Hi daddy!' she called.

'Hi pumpkin,' he called back.

Alice jumped up and began to put the food on the table as her parents took off their wet coats and boots.

Kennedy Bloom came into the room, dirty with engine grease. 'Have I got time for a quick shower?'

'No,' said Alice. 'I made dinner. Come and sit down.'

She poured tea for the three of them.

'How was your day?' asked her mother.

Alice shrugged. 'Boring. School. Played for a bit. Got soaked. How about you?'

Martha looked tired and stressed. 'It was long. This weather brings everyone inside, whether they really need it or not. Malia called in sick, so there were just two of us.'

Alice's mother ran a kind of soup kitchen and cafe for the poor and homeless. People payed whatever they could afford. If they could't afford anything, they didn't pay anything. Mostly, it was run as a charity, so her mother spent a lot of her free time fundraising and taking in donations of food.

Alice sometimes helped out in the holidays when it was very busy, but she didn't much like to. It was depressing.

Her dad was eating. He worked long days at the garage and was always hungry. He'd been out for 12 hours today. Often he was later, and Alice and her mother ate without him. On warm summer evenings, she would walk the mile or so to the garage to take him a shopping bag filled with sandwiches, fruit, and a tupperware dish of warm food, so that he could stay later and get more done.

She worried about him, and often lay awake in bed listening for the familiar bang of the front door that meant he was home.

Now, he heaped up bread with ham and egg, and smiled at her. 'Thanks for having dinner ready. I'm starving.'

'Did you hear about the Christmas Village competition?' said Alice. 'They told us about it at school.'

'I heard about it,' said Kennedy,' but it costs a lot of money.'

'Not if everyone does their bit. My teacher said if everyone begins at home, and works outwards, we could make a difference.'

'The only thing that makes a difference round here is money,' said her mother, pouring herself another cup of tea. 'There's a reason why Hogweed Fields never wins anything.'

'It's because we never try,' said Alice. 'If we won £50,000, we could have a new playground.'

'Believe me, darling, if this village won £50,000, a new playground would be the least of their priorities. Sunny Meadows is bound to win, anyway. they always do.'

Alice sighed. 'Sometimes I hate being from Hogweed Fields. I hate being poor.'

'There's more to life than money,' said her dad. 'We have each other, we have our health, and we have everything we need. As you get older, these are the things that are important.'

'But I'm not old. I'm ten. I want a playground to play in.'

'Finish your food, and get your homework done.'

'But I already did do it,' protested Alice.

'Alright,' said her mother, disbelieving.

The next day was Saturday. Alice's mother woke her before she left for work and gave her her instructions for the day. They couldn't afford babysitters for her, so she always went to work with them when she was little. Now she was older, she was allowed to do her own thing a bit more.

Alice made herself a bowl of cereal and watched TV in her pyjamas for a while. Then she put on jeans and a jumper and brushed her hair.

She liked days with no school, days with hours and hours of glorious freedom stretching ahead. She cut two large pieces of chocolate cake and wrapped them in tin foil.

She pulled on second-hand pink suede boots and went outside, slamming the front door behind her to make it lock automatically.

Her dad's garage was on the edge of the village, away from the shops. She liked to walk there, because she loved nature, and it was a very green and grassy walk , lined with trees.

Franklin's Garage was on a large plot of land, it's main building set back from the road. The building was black and faded, with its name in ancient lettering across the front.

Franklin wasn't her dad's name, but if people called him it, as they often did, he answered, and never bothered to correct them.

The garage had been there for decades, and no-one seemed to remember who the original Franklin actually was, or if he ever existed at all.

Alice loved the yard, with its hulks of old cars and discarded parts. It was dirty and dusty and there were lots of places to hide and play. She had grown to love the smell of oil and petrol.

Her dad was working when she arrived, but, as always, he was happy to see her.

'I brought you some cake,' said Alice, holding out her foil parcel.

'Thanks, sweetie.'

He sat on an old wooden bench, and she sat beside him.

'Share?' he said.

'Okay.'

They ate cake together, looking out the wide front doors onto the wintry day. Leaves whirled lazily around the yard, dancing up and down gently in the breeze.

'What are you up to today?' asked Kennedy.

'I don't know. I really want to do the Christmas thing.'

'What Christmas thing?'

'The competition I told you about.'

'It's not really something you can do on your own, Alice.'

'Maybe people will help.'

He hugged her with one arm. 'You're always so positive.'

'Can I stay and help?'

'Okay, for a little while. You can sweep up and answer the phones, and I'll pay you with sweets later.'

Alice thought that if she grew up to work with her dad at the garage, that wouldn't be the worst thing.

Chapter Ten

It was a long walk to the other end of the village where her mother worked. Alice didn't rush. She liked walking through the streets in the drizzle, looking in shop windows and waving at people she knew.

She went into a story in her head that there was a zombie apocalypse and she was the only child left. The adults respected her as a strong warrior and, even though she was only ten, they made her their leader. They nicknamed her 'wolf girl', because she was wild and a survivor. She found some bubblegum flavoured chewing gum in her pocket, and she put it into her mouth, pretending it was the only sustenance she'd had for days.

On the way, she bumped into a group of friends from school. They talked for a while, and her best friend Melanie decided to come to the cafe with her.

The weather had driven everyone inside again, and her mother was very busy behind the counter.

'Can we help?' said Melanie.

'Oh, great! Can you cut some more bread please? Alice, can you clear tables?'

Alice hated clearing tables. She frowned as Melanie put on a plastic hat and gloves behind the counter and moved to the bread counter. The knife was huge next to the small girl, but she cut expertly. Alice's friends had ended up helping a lot when they came to hang out with her. They usually got paid in hot chocolate, and they were fine with that.

Alice started with the empty tables near her, collecting bowls, plates and cups. She was a pretty clumsy girl and dropped as many as made it to the sink, but at least she was trying.

She tried to avoid the homeless people, because they scared her a bit. There was something so sad and desperate about them. It made her feel helpless and sick.

After a while, the cafe emptied out except for one or two stragglers. Alice's mother gave them sandwiches and fruit to take away for dinner as they left.

Sometimes Alice worried about her mother being robbed, but her customers were always polite and generous to her. Sometimes they brought her little presents to say thank you, and she always cried on those days.

Once the place had quietened down, Alice and Melanie wiped down tables as the adults cleaned the kitchen and counters.

In the far corner was an old man, finishing his cup of tea. He smiled at Alice, and his face was pleasant and kind. He wore a grubby Santa hat on top of short white hair.

Alice moved through the tables towards him.

'I like your hat,' she said.

'Thankyou.' He smiled at her again.

'It isn't Christmas yet, though.'

'Someone gave it to me,' he said. 'When you're in my position, you take what you can get. Doesn't have to be fashionable or seasonal.'

Alice put down her cloth and spray and sat in a chair at the next table.

'I know how you feel,' she said. 'My clothes are always second-hand, too.'

'Clothes are clothes,' said the man. 'As long as you're comfortable and warm, that's all you need them for.'

'My name is Alice.'

'Good to meet you, Alice. My name is George.' He held out a hand wearing grubby fingerless gloves. Alice paused, then reached over and shook it briefly.

'Alice, don't be bothering George,' called her mother.

'I'm not,' she called back. She rolled her eyes. 'How come when adults talk it's called talking, but if children talk, it's called bothering?'

'Well, luckily, I don't mind being bothered.'

'Did you hear about the Christmas competition?' she asked George.

He said he hadn't, so she told him about it. 'My dad said it would cost too much money, though,' she said.

George thought for a moment. 'Last year, I was dreading Christmas,' he said. 'I have no children, no home. Watching families out shopping together, throwing money at their children or at family members who don't even like them, it made me sad. When I was a child, we went to church, we sang carols in the street, we spent weeks making decorations. When the Christmas carol sheets came out in the school assembly, there was a buzz in the air. I still remember they were purple, with a picture of the Nativity on. It was exciting. It was *magical*. People were nice to each other.'

Alice nodded. 'We still have sheets like that, but ours are red.'

George nodded, too. 'So you understand what I mean?'

'What will you do at Christmas?' she asked.

'God willing, I'll come here, just like I did last year. I got a hot meal, some good company. I got thick socks, a razor and a bar of soap. When I left, there was a bright star in the sky, and I said a quick prayer of gratitude for places like this. It was a good day.'

Alice felt a new respect for her mother. Alice had always complained about her not being there on Christmas night, plus she'd always refused to come and help.

'My point is,' said George, 'don't forget what Christmas is about. There's more to it than money. If you want to enter this competition, then use your imagination, use your brains, and use the friends around you. That's what makes you rich.'

After George had left, Alice and Melanie sat at a table with Martha and they all had lunch together. Melanie's parents were working all day as well. Sometimes they went to visit Melanie's mother in the supermarket and got free samples of fudge or cheese or whatever was on offer that day.

Alice told them her ideas for Christmas.

'I won't have time to help,' said her mum. 'I'm already far too busy.'

'Maybe other people will help.'

'My dad is a builder,' said Melanie. 'He could do something.'

'See?' said Alice to her mother. 'I'm going to plan it out tonight.'

'Have you done your homework yet?'

'Of course,' she lied. 'You need to trust me more.'

She grinned at her mother.

Chapter Eleven

The next day, Alice skipped school, which she did often. It wasn't something she was proud of, but it was something she did often.

Her parents didn't notice, as they were always at work early. She had set up an email account with her mother's name, and she emailed school her excuses from that.

She was savvy enough to lie low so she wasn't spotted, so she filled her pockets with snacks and headed off to the playground.

Although it was called a playground by the village children, it was more of a waste ground. A couple of rusty swings, a slide, and a roundabout that no longer went round. Officially, it had been condemned as dangerous, but it had been abandoned for so long that eventually, one by one, the children started coming back.

When Alice got there, two other girls she vaguely knew from another school were there. She offered to share her sweets, and the three of them sat on the tarmac together.

'We're talking about a mystery,' said one of the girls. Her name was Ashley, and she was here at the park very often. Her friend was called Amber, which didn't at all suit her dark complexion and tough-girl exterior. Alice thought she should be a redhead, or at least an warm auburn brown.

'I'm good at mysteries,' said Alice. 'Maybe I can help.'

'Some weird stuff has been going on,' said Ashley. 'A couple of girls we know have just disappeared, and no-one seems to care.'

'What do you mean disappeared?'
'No-on has seen them for days, and their families are all telling conflicting stories. We think it's suspicious.'
'Do the police know?"
'Everyone is acting like they don't know anything,' said Amber. 'It hasn't been on the news or anything.'
'Who are the girls?'
'Amanda Foster and Jeannie La Mer.'
'I don't think I know them.'
'We think the women know something about it.'
'What women?'
'Have you heard of the WI?'
'Yeah, they meet in my mum's cafe.'
'We think they are some kind of secret society.'
'No, they just bake and crochet and stuff. Last week they were making art out of old books. My mum told me. She joined in for a while when it was quiet.'

Ashley looked around and lowered her voice. 'Before Caroline disappeared, she was being really mean to Amanda. She was saying bad things about Amanda's mum. They had a big fight. Pulling each other's hair and everything. I saw one of the old women there. She wrote something down in a little book. A few days later, they were gone.'

'Wow. Maybe I can help. Next time they meet, I could try to listen in.'
'That would be cool.'
I'll meet you back here next week, same time.'
The girls agreed.
'What was your name again?' asked Amber.
'Alice,' said Alice. 'Alice Bloom.'

Walking to the shops later, she bumped into a tall, thin woman carrying a large handbag. She was holding the bag in front of her, rummaging in it, and at the same time, trying to stop several items from being dislodged and falling out. A brown velvety scarf, a large brown purse with a showy gold clasp on it, and a diary stuffed with papers were in danger of escaping entirely onto the pavement.

'Oh, where is it, where is it, where is it?' muttered the woman before colliding with Alice. The diary made a leap for it and Alice caught it deftly in her left hand.

The woman glanced up, gratefully.

'Oh, thank you, Nancy dear. I'm such a scatterbrain, I can't imagine where I've left it.'

Alice stood, holding out the diary.

'Well, she'll be furious if it's gone for good. She already thinks I can't be trusted with anything.'

She looked up at Alice.

'The WI minutes from last week's meeting. I'm supposed to be typing them up.' She took the diary and stuffed it back in her huge bag.

'My name is Alice,' said Alice.

The woman paled. 'What?'

'I'm Alice. I don't think you know me. You might know my mum, though.'

The woman froze for a moment. 'I'm so sorry. I must be mistaken.' She looked around. 'Please don't tell anyone,' she hissed, and rushed off down the street.

Alice watched her go but she didn't turn round or look back, although the stiff set of her neck and shoulders implied she wanted to.

Alice shrugged and turned to carry on. There really were some crazy old ladies around these days.

And then on the floor, at her feet, she saw a piece of paper. It must have come out of the falling diary.
It had names on it. It had *her* name on it.

SM	HF
Devon Lite	Max Lite
Carrie-Ann Foster	Amanda Foster
Marguerite La Mer	Jeannie La Mer
Kitty Harriet	Joanna Harriet
Nancy Bloom	Alice Bloom

She picked it up and stuffed it in her pocket.
Shortly after school hours were finished, Alice's friends met her in the woods at the edge of the village, not far from her dad's garage. They liked to climb up high in the trees, where they could watch the world go by and talk about things without adults listening in all the time.

Even ten year olds like privacy sometimes.
There were six other children there by 4 o'clock. They sat and watched men and vehicles piling into the fields across the boundary line in Sunny Meadows.
'Building something,' said one boy, Carl, as they pulled lengths of timber from the back of a truck.
'Genius,' said Alice.
'Well, what do you think it is?' he demanded.
'I don't know.' said Alice. 'Who cares, anyway?'
Another car had arrived and a large man with a huge moustache had rolled himself out and strode into the middle of things. They couldn't hear what he was saying, but by his arm gestures, he seems to be telling people what to do.
'Maybe it's the fair,' said a girl called Tiffany, excitedly. 'Maybe it's the fair setting up. Or a circus.'

'We wouldn't be allowed to go anyway,' said Alice. 'Not to Sunny Meadows.'

'We could sneak in the back,' said Carl.

'Why should we have to sneak in the back?' said Tiffany, 'and all the rich kids get to go in the front?'

'That's just the way it is,' sighed Alice.

She thought about George, and how happy he was to have a bar of soap and somewhere to go, and she felt ashamed of herself.

'We're not exactly poor,' she said.

'Speak for yourself,' said Carl. 'I didn't even have lunch today.'

Alice gave him some sweets from her pocket, and he took them, happily.

After her friends started to drift off home, she decided to walk to her dad's garage. It was getting dark, and she hoped she could walk home with him.

When she got there, she saw a lot of vehicles on the track, and her dad in the yard arguing with some men. She ran the rest of the way to his side, but he was already ordering the men off the property.

He was very angry and upset once they'd left.

'What's happened?' she asked him.

'Come inside,' he said. 'I need to call your mother.'

Chapter Twelve

That evening, Alice sat on the stairs and listened in to her parents' conversation. It was something she did often, even though she knew it was wrong. There is an old saying that eavesdroppers rarely hear any good about themselves. She had learned it to be true on many occasions.

'The track and most of the yard are in Sunny Meadows. They showed me the county plans. The boundary was moved in 1971, but no-one bothered to do anything about it. Until now.'

'Why now?' said Martha. She sounded upset.

'Because I tried to stop them building their stupid Christmas village too near the grounds. I thought it might be bad for business. Well, it will be now. They've blocked the road completely.'

'That has to be against the law.'

'It probably is, but who's going to take my side? I can't afford a solicitor. I wouldn't win anyway.'

'Why is it so important to them? They don't need the money.'

'They don't want the money. They just want to win, and forget the cost.'

Alice's mother sounded like she was crying.

'What will this mean?' she said.

'It means no money coming in over Christmas. After that, who knows?'

Alice ran down the stairs and threw her arms around her mother.

'It'll be okay,' she said. 'We'll figure it out. Don't cry.'

'Alice, you shouldn't have been listening in,' said her dad.

She hugged her dad, too. 'We'll be okay, won't we?'

'We'll do our best,' said her dad. 'I can still work if I can go out to people's cars rather than them come to me.'

'And maybe we can do the Christmas competition and win £50,000,' said Alice.

Her father kissed her head. 'Maybe,' he said.

A few days later, Alice and her friends were hanging out in the woods again, watching the progress at the farm.

It was fast work, and the wooden buildings were taking shape.

'It looks like Disneyland,' said one of the boys. 'Wonder if they'll keep it up after Christmas?'

'Probably not,' said Alice. 'Probably spend more than £50,000 on the whole thing, then they'll throw it all away.'

'That isn't what Christmas is about,' said Melanie.

There was a cracking sound from a nearby tree, then the sound of something dropping.

'Spies!' shouted Alice. 'Get them!'

The boys and girls slid down from the trees, and ran in the direction of the noise. There was no sign of anyone, but they continued to chase, after a while simply enjoying the race until they all stopped, worn out, and laughing.

There was no computer or internet at home, so Alice went to the library to do her research. She was on a mission.

She took Melanie with her to take notes. 'Like a secretary', she told her.

Alice set up at one of the computer tables, and the girls pulled up another table and chair for Melanie. They had several notebooks and pencils, a sketch pad, and Melanie had her dad's old phone. They looked very professional.

'I have an idea,' said Alice, switching on the monitor. 'A big idea.'

'I love your big ideas,' said Melanie. 'They are always fun.'

'This may be more work than fun. How would you like to beat Sunny Meadows for once?'

'I would love that!'

'I think a lot of people would.'

'First things first,' said Alice. 'The Plan.'

She started typing into the search engine, and Melanie watched, intrigued.

They didn't notice the librarian, who watched surreptitiously from behind the stacks while pretending to arrange the books.

Mrs Harriet was the kind of woman that no-one paid much attention to. It made her a good watcher.

Chapter Thirteen

Alice made sure to go to school, to do her homework, and to be the best girl that she could be to the outside world.

When you want huge favours and to be allowed a huge amount of leeway from your parents, it is best to be very good beforehand.

She had made her plans, and had begun to design posters to put up around the village.

On Friday afternoon, she went to the cafe and put a poster in the front window.

'What are you up to?' said her mother from behind the counter.

'There might be a few people coming in,' said Alice, sticking the edges down with pink tape.

'What do you mean? What are you up to?'

Martha went outside to read the poster.

'What is this?'

'I'm organising a Christmas committee,' said Alice. 'I want to do the competition.'

'Oh, Alice, don't you think we have more important things to do?'

'But we're not,' she said. 'We're not doing anything, are we?'

'Alice, you know we can't afford a solicitor. There's nothing we can do until after Christmas.'

'No, there are things we can do, and they don't need money. It's like George said about the carol sheets.'

'I have no idea what you're talking about,' said her mother, impatiently.

Just then her father arrived. 'Is everything okay?' he asked his wife. 'I got a message to meet Alice here.'

'Everything's fine, daddy,' said Alice. 'Come and sit down. I'm up to something.'

Just then, several of Alice's school friends burst through the door, many followed by their parents.

'They're coming!' said Alice, and to her parents, 'You should maybe start making some coffee. It might get busy in here.'

Alice was a very good public speaker and she held the attention of the room well as she laid out her plans, standing atop a dining table with her friends sitting at her feet.

'So you see,' she concluded, 'it's like George said. We may not have the money to throw at the competition like Sunny Meadows does, but we are rich in other ways. In Hogweed Fields, we have had to work for everything we have ever had, and that is the key. We don't have money, but we have skills, strength, hard work and spirit. I really believe we can do this.'

She looked at the faces in front of her. Melanie gave her a double thumbs up. Her parents looked proud.

'Sounds good to me,' said Kennedy, and Alice beamed with pride. If her dad was in, then others would follow.

At the back of room, the tall, thin woman that Alice had met earlier in the day was scribbling frantically into a thick notebook. Alice remembered the piece of paper in her pocket that she had picked up off the floor.

George had made his way from his usual corner table to congratulate her.

'I'm a bit nervous about how much of this plan is hinging on me,' he confided. 'What if I can't do it?'

'You'll be great,' said Alice. 'You're the only one who can do it. We are counting on you.'

George nodded. 'No pressure, then.'

Everyone was talking, or getting coffee, or sneaking out the door unnoticed. Several people had left before Alice saw a small boy with dark hair sitting alone by the door.

She nudged Melanie. 'Who is that kid?'

'I have no idea. Haven't seen him around before.'

The boy was small in size, but his eyes were intelligent. Alice thought he was probably what is meant by street smart. She caught his eye and smiled.

'He looks about our age.'

No sooner had they spotted the boy than he noticed them looking and shot straight out of the door and away down the street.

'Scares easily,' said Melanie, shrugging.

'I know, right?'

'Must have been your beautiful face.'

The girls laughed and went to get drinks for themselves.

Chapter Fourteen

They had a Christmas party in the cafe one night. All the villagers who came brought food and drink to share with the customers.

Everyone had updates and pictures of their work so far on the competition.

Kennedy Bloom had converted an old shell of a vehicle into a Santa's sleigh, and local carpenters were carving reindeers for the school children to paint.

A huge metal tree had been sculpted out of scrap and everyone in the village had donated one item to be hung from it to represent their family. They called it a 'community wish tree', which was Melanie's contribution.

Alice and Carl walked around the cafe, making sure everyone was having fun and had enough to eat.

They spotted George at his usual table and planted themselves in front of him. There was an elderly lady at the table as well. He didn't seem to happy to have been interrupted.

'This is Lady,' said George, grumpily. 'These are some kids.'

'Is that your real name?' said Carl. 'Like the dog in the film?'

Alice nudged him.

'George, I need to talk to you about your role,' she said.

'You are playing a role,' said Lady. 'On TV?'

'No, he's going to be our Santa.'

'Maybe,' said George.

'No, definitely,' said Alice. 'We can't do it without him.'

'Are you two girlfriend and boyfriend?' Carl asked Lady.

Alice kicked him under the table.

A few days later, she met up with Amber and Ashley at the park to talk about what they had discovered.

Alice showed them the piece of paper.

'What does it mean?' said Amber.

'All the names are matched up to others with the same last name.'

'Some of these are the ones that went missing,' said Ashley.

'What does it mean?' asked Amber again.

'I don't know,' said Alice, 'but I don't like that my name is on it. And more importantly, who is Nancy Bloom?'

'Oh my goodness,' said Ashley. 'I think I know.'

She pulled a piece of wadded up newspaper from her pocket. 'Someone asked me to give this to you.'

She handed it to Alice.

'Who did?'

'A little kid. He was grubby, with dark hair. He asked if I knew you.'

Alice unfolded the newspaper. It was a photo of three people, smiling into the camera, with a caption underneath.

Mayor Horatio, Veronica and Nancy Bloom enjoy a night out at the Sunny Meadows school Nativity.

Chapter Fifteen

The group of women seemed to take up the whole room.

There were only seven of them, and they tucked themselves away at a large table in the far window, but the rest of the cafe remained empty. They gave off an air of being unapproachable and important.

Even Alice's mother made herself scarce once she had served coffee and cakes, taking herself off into the storeroom to 'sort stuff'.

She took Alice with her, despite her protests.

'I hate the storeroom. It's dark and dusty and it makes me sneeze.'

Alice's mother sat her on a crate and gave her a list of stock and a pen. 'Just tick it off and make sure it's correct as I call things out.'

'What if a customer comes in? I should man the counter.'

'No-one is going to come in.'

'How do you know?'

'Hush. Now, 2kg coffee cans, 3 and a half. Tick it off.'

It was twenty minutes later before Alice managed to excuse herself to go to the bathroom.

She left the storeroom with strict instructions to go straight to the bathroom and then come straight back.

Naturally, she headed straight for the shop counter.

The women were talking too quietly to hear them from across the room. Alice got herself a glass of water, and after a second thought, got one for her mother as well.

There were empty coffee cups on the table, and untouched cakes. Alice didn't know what kind of person would ignore cakes, especially the pink frosted ones that were the cafe's speciality.

There were also sheets of paper laid out everywhere. The thin, nervous woman was there again, scribbling notes.

Alice remembered something.

The nervous woman looked up first and seemed even more worried than usual. The other woman followed her gaze and looked at Alice. It was hardly a warm, fuzzy feeling to have their cold, icy, unwelcoming eyes on her.

Alice smiled at them all and held out something to the tall woman.

'You dropped this.'

The women looked at the folded piece of paper in Alice's hand.

What?' whispered the woman in a faint voice.

'Mrs Trott?' said a woman with a vague accent. 'What is this?'

Alice focused her gaze on Mrs Trott. The woman looked terrified.

'The other day,' said Alice. 'When you called me Nancy. Remember?'

Mrs Trott shook her head. 'I don't remember…'

'I'm Alice.' She paused. 'My name is on this paper.'

The women seemed to recover themselves and the one nearest took the paper from Alice's hand.

'Thankyou, young lady,' said a pudgy lady in a large beige hat that made her look a bit like a mushroom. 'Now, if you just go back to your mother, we have things to discuss.' She smiled, small teeth glittering. It was a smile that was grotesque rather than pleasant, as if it wasn't very much at home on her face.

'Why is my name on there?' asked Alice.

'That's rather arrogant of you,' said the cold-eyed lady with the accent. 'It's hardly an uncommon name.'

Just then Alice's mother appeared at her side.

'Alice. Storeroom, now!'

'I just came to clear the cups....'

'Now!'

Alice scuttled off obediently, but feeling triumphant. The mystery was growing.

Chapter Sixteen

Ashley and Amber were already at the park when they arrived. They were on the rusty swings with another girl called Molly, who Alice knew from school. The chains of the swings creaked ominously every time they moved even a little bit.

Alice was with Melanie, Carl and a friend of Carl's called Jordy. Alice had never heard that name before and suspected he had completely made it up.

The children gathered on the broken roundabout. It didn't move round any more, but it was a good enough place to sit.

It was a chilly day, but Melanie had brought peppermints to keep everyone happy. They sat and shared as they discussed everything that had been going on in town.

'What do you know about the Wives Institute?' asked Alice.

'The women's group?' said Amber. 'My mum used to be one of them. She left because they found out some of them were having secret meetings without the others.'

'My dad says they are like the Masons, but for women,' said Carl.

'Don't they just knit and bake and stuff?' asked Ashley. 'Last year they donated all the cakes for the school fete.'

'Maybe in other towns,' agreed Alice, 'but here they seem strange and suspicious. One woman, Mrs Trott - she seems to be scared to death of something.'

'At least no other children have gone missing.'

'Except Kelly.'

The children all looked at Jordy.

'Who's Kelly,' said Alice.

Jordy shrugged. 'Who *was* Kelly, you mean. She went to my school. All of a sudden, she just vanished..'

'You mean she's missing? Are the police looking for her?'

'No-one is looking, not even her parents. They said she went to live with her grandmother for a while.'

'So, maybe she did.'

'Really?' Jordy was enjoying his time in the spotlight. 'What if I told you I know for a fact that she doesn't even have a grandmother?'

'How would you know that?'

'That's irrelevant. Besides, our teacher said she went to boarding school in Switzerland.'

'But wouldn't her parents know that?' said Melanie.

'You'd think so, wouldn't you?'

Suddenly, Amber shouted, 'Spies! Over there!' She pointed to the trees at the edge of the playground.

'Get them!'

The children leapt to their feet, as only children can, and were gone in a flash, racing across the dirty concrete and into the bushes.

The spy or spies were ready for them, though, and had moved away just as quickly. It was slow moving through the bushes and trees and became prickly and brambly the deeper they went.

After a while, the children gave up the chase and began to trickle off to their respective homes.

Chapter Seventeen

December flew by in swirls of golden leaves and flurries of soft snow.

Days got colder and jumpers got thicker, and it was a brave soul who left the house without hats or gloves.

Alice's gloves were unravelling a little at the fingertips from the winter before, but at least she had some.

It upset her to see so many visitors to the cafe with red, numb fingers which they squeezed tight around hot white cups to warm them up.

Eventually, she gave her gloves away. She told her mum that she'd lost them and kept her hands in her pockets whenever she could.

Winter is a hard time for the poor, no matter where they are. It was certainly no different in villages like Hogweed Fields, where poverty was the order of the day.

Very little money was coming in to the Bloom household that month. Alice's father worked when and where he could, but things were difficult.

Alice's mother was very busy at the restaurant , but she was so kind-hearted that she gave away more than she brought in.

By mid-December, the school holidays arrived, and the days became darker and darker until soon night began creeping down at around 4pm.

Alice stayed home in the daytime when her parents were at work. Sometimes she had friends round to play for a few hours, and sometimes they went outside to play if the weather wasn't too bad.

She tried to be good for her parents, and so sometimes she tidied the house and did dishes, and sometimes she made simple dinners for them to come home to after their long, cold days at work. She didn't like doing it, but she did it anyway, because maybe it would make their days a little bit easier.

Alice and her friends used their spare time to keep up work on the Christmas competition. They drew designs of what they envisioned and wrote long lists - some a little bit far-fetched, but it never hurts to dream big.

A poor community is often a community of skilled workers, and carpenters, electricians, builders and painters were just what the committee needed.

'The rich tell people what to do, and the poor people do,' George had told Alice, cynically.

Alice had nodded, solemnly. They would do, and they would win, too.

The adults were on board as well. Hand-made decorations crept up all over the village, beautiful images made from wood and metal, and lovingly painted in dark living rooms and kitchens on chilly nights.

Several of the women, led by the Wives Institute no doubt, made it their mission to knit, crochet and patchwork festive blankets, jumpers, hats, scarves and gloves to give away at the charity cafe. They even made smaller ones for dogs, cats and outdoor pets like guinea pigs and rabbits.

Alice walked down the lane one day, admiring the decorations and shop windows. The village was looking better than ever, despite the hunger and worry that existed behind locked doors. Alice hoped they would win some money to ease those things. They had put in their application to the competition that any money won would go straight back to the community.

Christmas was really in the air now that schools had broken up and the days were counting down in single numbers. It was just over a week until the big day. Alice knew there wouldn't be a lot of money for gifts, but she couldn't help being caught up in the excitement and the magic, and to secretly hope that Santa would bring them a miracle and make everything okay.

Speaking of Santa, she had persuaded a reluctant George to play the part.

'I'm too thin and grouchy to be Father Christmas,' he complained.

'Oh, shush,' Alice had said. 'You're perfect. You just need some stuffing and a bigger beard. Besides, have you got anything better to do?'

Then she gave him her sweetest smile and a peppermint, and he grumpily gave in.

During her walk through the village, she stopped in front of one particular window in awe. It was breathtaking.

The window of the grocer's shop had been decorated as though it were straight out of Victorian times.

A wooden doll's house and wooden rocking horse sat unpainted on either side of the display. A tiny pine tree had been cut down from the woods and decorated with handmade figures and striped candy canes. Bunches of holly and mistletoe covered the window, and plates of oranges, chocolates, plum puddings and chestnuts were gathered around the tree.

She saw her own reflection among them, a small, skinny girl with a cloud of dark hair, and her eyes shining bright with magic.

Alice remembered the story of the Little Match Girl, the hungry little girl whose matches showed her warmth and food and family, so we wouldn't be alone at the end of her short life.

She was as hungry as that little girl, but for more than food. She wanted more for her family, for her community. She was hungry for life to be fair and give them the chances that other people had.

After a moment, Alice noticed another ghostly face beside her in the window. It was the little boy from the meeting, his dark eyes scared and wide.

Alice turned to him and he panicked and tried to run, but she grabbed him.

'You! You gave the newspaper to Amber. Why are you spying on me?'

'Let me go!' They tussled for a while, but Alice was much stronger.

'Who are you?' she demanded. 'What do you want?'

The little boy stopped resisting, and sighed. 'My name is Max,' he whispered. 'I need to talk to you. But we can't let them hear us.'

'Talk about what?' said Alice.

Max leaned closer. 'About Nancy,' he whispered. 'And the others.'

Alice was surprised. 'Okay, come with me.'

She took him to the dilapidated playground, mainly because they were no other adult-free places to go to.

Along the way, Max told her a little bit about himself.

'I'm kind of on the run right now. My parents aren't really looking for me. They don't like me much. They might not have even noticed I've gone. They tend to forget about me sometimes.'

'Who are you running from?'
'Lots of people. Everyone. Kids are disappearing.'
'Yeah, we've noticed. Are you from here?'
'I'm from Hogweed Fields. Been here my whole life.'
'Me too.'
'It sucks.'
'I know.'

At the playground, they sat on the creaky swings that were nearest to one another, so they could speak quietly. Alice got a good look at her new friend. He was very small, although he swore he was nine years old. Alice wasn't too sure about that.

Max had a grubby little heart-shaped face, big dark eyes, and dark hair which looked like it hadn't seen a comb in a long time. He wore a fleecy coat which looked pretty warm, but he sat hunched up and shivering.

'Tell me what you know,' said Alice, kindly. He seemed scared to death.

'It all started when I was rummaging around at home for some change to get sweets with. I found a box of pictures in a cupboard. They were of my family, but a bit different. I saw a picture of me, but then I realised it wasn't me. I thought maybe I had a brother I didn't know about.

'My mum gets drunk a lot, and she was drunk then. I asked her about the photo. At first she told me to shut up, but later that night she started to talk. And that's when I learned about Devon.'

'Your brother?'

'Devon wasn't my brother. he was kind of…..me.'

'I don't get it.'

'He lived in Sunny Meadows. I ran away to investigate, but he was missing. Lots of others were missing, too. And I saw people there, but they weren't them.'

'Seriously, Max, I don't understand.'

'I saw you there.'

Alice sneered. 'I've never been to Sunny Meadows in my life!'

'And neither had she - Nancy - even been to Hogweed Fields. That's why you have never seen each other. I picked up the newspaper photo there.'

'Who is Nancy?'

'She's you, but different.'

'Different how?'

'Her hair is different. She's quiet. She only goes out with parents. And she's *rich*.'

'How rich?'

'*Really* rich. She has a mansion, a huge car, *staff*.'

'Wow. That could have been me.'

'Maybe, just maybe, it *should* be you.'

'What do you mean Max?'

'Kids are going missing, Alice, and each of those kids has a twin in a different village. So, who's it going to be, Alice? You or her?'

'Her!'

'So what are we going to do about it?'

Chapter Eighteen

In Sunny Meadows that night, there was a meeting held in a dark, shadowy basement.

'You will notice I have called this meeting in Francine's absence,' said Veronica Bloom.

The other ladies nodded nervously, and tried not to glance at Francine's empty seat in case she could somehow see them through it.

Mrs Trott's empty seat was quiet and unnoticed, just as she herself had been for much of her life.

'I'm not sure how comfortable I feel about this,' said Mrs Blatch. Her fat handbag was clutched anxiously in her lap.

'I understand your concern, but I think we have to all agree that Francine is getting out of control.'

'She isn't playing by the rules,' agreed Marilyn Foster. 'This is supposed to be a game, not life and death.'

'Is this because she voted Nancy for dissimilation?' said Mrs Blatch, quietly.

'Of course not,' said Veronica. 'Nancy is a good girl. There is no question of dissimilation. Alice, on the other hand, is proving to be a bit of a problem.'

'You can't just choose your favourite, Mrs Bloom.'

'I understand that, Mrs Blatch, and at this point, winning is not my objective. I am more worried about our real identities becoming known. This was a foolish game that we came up with for our own entertainment, at the risk of the children, the community, and the wider world. Francine is becoming unpredictable and power-hungry.'

'We are also running out of storage for those we have dissimilated,' said Mrs Harriet. 'I didn't realise there would be so many.'

'Well, we can always wake them up if necessary, or dispose of them.'

'What are you suggesting? That we call off the game?'

'I'm suggesting that we end the game. Back to the start.'

'Start again with the children, you mean?'

'I mean back to the start *before* the children, before the villages, before we even arrived here. I mean we end it before anyone gets hurt. We stop this now.'

The women looked around at each other in the flickering candlelight. The same question was on every face.

Who was going to stop Francine La Mer?

Part Three - The Bloom Girls

Chapter Nineteen

For the first time in her life, Alice felt afraid.

She wasn't afraid of physical danger, or of the darkness ahead, or the unknown. For the first time ever, Alice was afraid of letting her parents down.

She pulled the door closed behind her as quietly as possible, and stepped onto the dark path.

Max was waiting for her out on the road, his little dark figure standing out against the bright snow.

It was the middle of the night in Hogweed Fields, and there was no-one else around. The streets they walked down were empty, black and cold.

Alice still felt a little nervous, though. She felt uncomfortable with her heavy rucksack on her back, and she felt uncomfortable in her heart knowing how worried her mum and dad would be when they woke to find her gone.

Max was in good spirits. He had been on his own for so long that he was happy to have her company.

'Did you bring any food?' he asked her.

'Yeah. Are you hungry?'

'A little bit. But it can wait. We'd better not waste it.'

'How long do you think it'll take? I Googled it, but it was hard to tell using the roads.'

'A few hours. Do you have good shoes on?'

'No.'

'Oh, well, your feet might hurt then. My feet hurt when I walk a lot.'

'Yeah, mine too.'

'What food did you bring?'

'Sandwiches, chocolate, apples, cookies, and a flask of hot chocolate. You want something?'

'Maybe a sandwich. Well, maybe just half? For walking energy.'

Once they were out of sight of her house, Alice stopped to unzip her bag and dig out a sandwich half and a few cookies for him.

Max wolfed them down in just a few bites, but he seemed happy enough.

Alice wondered if he was so little because his parents didn't look after him. She wondered what else he'd gone without in life. Poverty was no reason not to be good parents.

She felt another twinge of guilt and sent a quick prayer up to the stars for her mum and dad to forgive her. They had always been good to her, and she hadn't always been so good in return.

'It'll be faster if we stick to the main roads, and probably safer,' she told him. 'I've been researching.'

'You've been researching running away from home?'

'I'm not running away from home, as such. I intend to go back eventually.'

Max looked disappointed. 'Oh, 'cause if you ran away for good, we could look after each other and stuff.'

'Don't worry,' said Alice. 'I won't ditch you once this is all over.'

They were approaching the main road, heading towards her dad's garage. Seeing the big dark building on the horizon made her feel sad.

'It's all so unfair,' she snapped.

'Life's unfair,' said Max, sagely. 'Deal with it.'

'I am dealing with it.'

Her anger only strengthened her resolve that she was doing the right thing. The people in Sunny Meadows got everything handed to them. Well, they were going to have to fight hard to beat Alice Bloom.

It was slow going on the thick snow, and both children had damp feet in no time. After an hour or so, they were all the way out by the outskirts of town.

A bright moon lit up a wide open space. It looked huge in its white snow-covered state. The only thing that marked off the road from the fields beside it was a muddy ditch on each side of the tarmac. They followed those dark lines until their eyes got used to the whiteness.

They came to a high signpost with four signs on it.

'I've never been out of Hogweed Fields before,' said Alice. 'I don't think so anyway.'

'Why not?'

'I don't know why not. Everything I've ever needed has been here.'

She looked at the signs. The road ahead led all the way to the city, just the idea of which was so exciting to the children. It may as well have been the road to Oz.

'We could keep walking and walking and walk all the way to the city,' said Max. 'I've never been that far. It would take days and days.'

The road to the left led to Gardenia Heights. Alice had seen it in magazines. It was filled with mansions owned by football players and local celebrities. There were expensive restaurants and designer stores.

The road to the right led to Sunny Meadows, that perfect suburban dream, the ideal place to build your life and raise your family.

Alice raised one grubby, worn little shoe and placed it on the road to Sunny Meadows. It felt like the biggest step she had ever taken in her whole life.

Several miles away, in her fluffy white bed in her warm, soft room, Nancy Bloom opened her eyes.
Something had happened. She didn't know what, but she felt it in every bit of her bones.

Closing the door of the black shed at the bottom of her garden, Veronica Bloom felt danger approaching.
Something had happened, and time was running out.
In a dark church basement lined with candles, Francine La Mer felt Alice crossing the boundary line.
Her eyes darkened with anger.

Chapter Twenty

It wasn't yet morning when Alice and Max arrived in the middle of the village, but the quality of the light was different.

Everything was clean and bright, street lamps worked perfectly, and Christmas lights were strung in zigzags across every street. Decorations were everywhere. and there were hanging baskets filled with holly and poinsettia.

In the village square itself, across from the beautiful 13th century church, was the largest Christmas tree either Alice or Max had ever seen in their whole lives. They stood at the foot of it, looking upwards at the lights, figures, bells and gifts.

'I'll bet that tree cost more than our entire competition entry,' said Alice, sadly. 'I don't know why we bothered to try.'

'Well, we might still have a chance,' said Max, hopefully.

'No.' Alice sighed. 'We don't. We might as well say goodbye to that prize money.'

Max affected an air of sadness, too. After what he deemed to be an appropriate moment of mourning, he asked, 'Is there any chocolate left?'

Alice handed him the rucksack and sat down at the base of the tree. He'd already eaten most of the food himself, and half of the sweets in her pocket. He particularly liked Raspberry Bombs which melted and fizzed when bitten into to.

'What now?' she asked.

'I don't know,' said Max, with a mouth full of chocolate. 'Maybe we should just rest for a bit.'

Alice looked across the square at the church. It's windows were lit, even at this early hour, a warm, orange, welcoming light.

'Okay,' she said. 'But not here. It's freezing.'

She took back the rucksack, which was much thinner and lighter than when they started out, thanks to Max's endless appetite. For a little guy, he could really put it away.

'Come on,' she said, pulling on his arm. 'Sanctuary.'

She was worried that the church may be locked, but as they approached, they could hear faint Christmas music drifting through from behind the heavy wooden door.

She stopped at the door, and looked back at Max. 'Shall we? Is it safe?'

He shrugged. 'Only one way to find out.'

Alice opened the door slowly, trying not to make it creak, but it creaked anyway, and very loudly. It seemed loud enough to wake the whole village.

'Shhhh,' said Max.

'Okay, okay.'

The church was beautiful inside, lit up red and gold with lights and decorations. Holly, ivy and ferns had been brought inside and filled the room with their earthy fragrances.

Shiny wooden pews stretched the length of the room and all the way up to the gleaming white altar.

The two children crept up the aisle, feeling both awed and afraid. Neither had been in such a beautiful room before.

'It's like Disneyland,' said Max, who had no idea what Disneyland looked like.

He felt very small in the midst of all the tall carvings, painting and coloured glass windows. He wondered if Jesus was angry with him for running away from home like he had.

The Christmas music stopped abruptly, as though a button had been pressed.

They both jumped with shock as a soft voice spoke from the far end of the pew nearest the altar.

'Good morning.'

An elderly lady was sitting on the bench with a dark blue, cloth-bound bible in her hands.

'Oh, hello,' said Alice, trying to act naturally. *Just a couple of kids, out for a 4am visit to church. No biggie.*

'I don't usually see anyone at this time of day,' said the lady. She placed her bible next to a pile of things beside her and stood up.

Alice took a step back slowly, putting a protective hand out to Max and pushing him behind her gently.

'Now, is there something I can help you children with?'

'We're here to visit family, but we are a little early,' said Alice. 'We thought we would wait in here and… pray…for a while.'

'And who would you be here to visit? Perhaps I know them.'

'My aunt. *Our* aunt.'

'Oh? How nice. What's her name?'

Neither Alice or Max answered.

The lady reached down beside her and picked up a pair of gold-rimmed glasses. She polished them and put them on.

'Ah, now I see you clearly, I think I may know exactly why you are here. You look like a girl I know. A very good little girl from right here in Sunny Meadows.

Now you,' she peered closer at Alice. 'Are you a good girl?'

She smiled and her small teeth gleamed in the light. Alice looked at the bench and saw the hat, the big hat that had reminded her of a mushroom when she had seen it in the cafe.

'She's one of them!' she screamed. 'Run, Max!' They turned for the door, but little Max was too slow, and the woman grabbed him.

He bit and kicked but she held on tight.

'Go, Alice,' he shouted. 'I can look after myself against an old bag! Get help! Everything you need to know is at the bottom of the garden.'

'I'll come back,' she yelled from the door. 'I promise.' And she flew out into the night, slamming the door behind her with a loud crash. This time she hoped it would wake up the whole village.

Chapter Twenty-One

Nancy woke up so early that it was still dark. She'd had a very restless sleep, filled with anxiety and bad dreams.

It took her a moment to realise it was the day of the Christmas competition.

Her heart sank, and she wondered if that was the source of her unrest. Visitors from all nearby villages would descend on Sunny Meadows that evening for the big reveal, Sunny Meadows would win, and everyone would hate them even more. And she would have to stand beside her parents, smiling, well-dressed, well-fed and privileged.

She wondered why everyone else even bothered to try, when the odds were consistently weighed so heavily against them.

She wondered what would happen if she just didn't bother to show up.

Something was flashing at her window. She watched it for quite a while, before she noticed it had some kind of pattern.

flashflashflash flash flash flash flashflashflash

The pattern repeated over an over with a little break in-between each sequence.

Nancy watched it for ages, wondering what it was. After a while, she slid out of her warm bed and over the thick carpet to the window.

There was a figure in the garden making the light. The flashes came from the figure and with each flash Nancy saw more of the person.

She switched on a lamp beside her, so the person could see her and waved to show she could see them too. She gestured to say she was coming down.

As Nancy pulled on her coat and boots, she was well aware that this was the most rebellious she had ever been in her life. She was't allowed outside before her parents woke, not even in the garden. But it felt right. Something told her that she was on the verge of something very important.

There had never been danger or excitement in the girl's life, and it made her feel exquisitely alive.

As Alice disappeared through the door, Max squirmed in the firm grip of Mrs Blatch.

'Get off me, you old boot.'

'Now, now,' said Mrs Blatch, sweetly. 'No need to be rude. I know exactly who you are and what you've been up to. We've been waiting to speak to you.'

'I didn't do anything,' said Max. 'Let me go home.'

'Oh, I'm afraid it's too late for that. Your parents have already been informed of your unfortunate demise. They weren't too bothered, to be honest.'

'You're lying,' shouted Max, with tears in his eyes.

He wriggled, but her hold on him was unyielding. She was ridiculously strong for a little old lady.

With her free hand she pulled out an ancient mobile phone and pressed a button.

'I've got one,' she said into the phone. 'And a nasty little one at that.'

Max felt a twinge of fear for the first time. He had spent months snooping around. He knew who she was calling and what they would do to him.

While she was distracted, he swung round and shoved her as hard as he could. She stumbled, and tripped backwards over Alice's discarded rucksack. Unfortunately, she pulled Max down with her. On the way, he twisted his arm painfully out of her grip. He felt a sharp pain and a snap, and his vision greyed slightly as the both hit the ground.

Mrs Blatch fell hard with a thump. Max, as most children do, immediately bounced back up.

The phone had skittered away across the altar, and lay there, glowing red and pulsating like a heart. Max leapt toward it, but retreated as a voice came booming out of it.

'STAY THERE, CHILD!'

He scooted back onto his bottom in shock.

'STAY THERE! DON'T YOU DARE RUN!'

Max, who had never in his life done as he was told, leapt to his feet and ran.

He heaved on the heavy front door, but it didn't budge. It was locked tight.

Chapter Twenty-Two

Alice and Nancy faced each other in the sparkling snow. There was electricity in the air.

Alice had come to fight, to make demands, to make things fair, but standing there, looking at her own face looking back from beneath a thick furry hood, she was overwhelmed with emotion.

'You look just like me,' she said.

'You must be Alice,' said Nancy. 'I feel like I've been seeing you my whole life.'

She held out her hand, and after a moment, Alice took it. They looked at their hands, which were the same.

'What is going on?' said Nancy.

Alice took a deep breath. I have a story to tell you, but it isn't safe out here. I think they are looking for me.'

'Come with me.'

In the safety of Nancy's dressing room, the two girls huddled under a warm duvet and told their stories. They were immediate co-conspirators and felt like they had been together their whole lives.

'I'm scared,' said Nancy. 'Why are so many children missing in both our villages? Is there a killer out there?'

Alice told her twin everything she had learned from Max.

'Something is going on, and it's to do with the women.'

'Which women?'

'The Wives Institute'

'My mum runs the Wives Institute in Sunny Meadows,' said Nancy.

'Really? Do you think she's one of them?'

'She's strict, but I don't think she'd hurt anyone.' Nancy thought hard. 'There was one day, though. I heard her talking about Carrie-Ann, then Carrie-Ann disappeared.'

'So maybe she is one of them.'

'What do we do?'

'We have to save Max.' Then, Alice remembered something. 'He said to tell you something! He said look at the bottom of the garden.'

'The bottom of the garden? Wait, I saw someone once, when I was down there, by the sheds.'

'What's in the sheds?'

'I don't know.'

'Shall we go and find out?'

They crept back out, into the dark hallway.

'Listen,' whispered Alice. 'Whatever we find, we're in this together. Deal?'

'Deal.'

Across the hallway, Veronica Bloom's eyes blazed as she listened behind her bedroom door.

Max raced from room to room, and there were a lot of them. Beyond the main chapel, the church was a maze of small dark rooms.

Max wondered if Mrs Blatch was up and about yet. He felt kind of bad about hurting her, even if she was evil.

He heard noise in the corridor behind him and ducked into the nearest room. It was filled with robes on railings. He crawled under them and made himself comfortable.

He hoped Alice would come back with help sometime soon. He was getting hungry already.

The row of black sheds loomed tall above the little girls. Alice rubbed her hand on a grubby window and looked inside one. It was the same one that had all its contents piled up outside, now covered in snow.

'The rest have storage and gardening stuff in,' said Nancy, 'but this one is suspicious.'

'It's locked,' said Alice.

Nancy was disappointed. 'I don't know where the key might be.'

'We don't need one,' said Alice. 'The lock is rubbish.'

She rummaged around through the pile of stuff in the snow until she found what she wanted, then she set to work on breaking open the lock.

Nancy was shocked. 'Alice, no, we'll get in trouble.'

'In case you haven't noticed, we are already in trouble. There!' Alice snapped the lock and pulled open the door.

'Where did you learn how to do that?'

'My dad. He's pretty cool.'

Nancy watched her go inside, impressed.

In the shed were several boxes, some lying down, some standing up. They had lids like coffins.

Alice went to the nearest one. It said 'Foster' on the lid. She opened it.

'Get in here, Nancy. You need to see this.'

'What is it?' Nancy looked inside the box, then screamed.

'Shhhhhh! They'll hear us. And we'll be next.'

Nancy clamped a hand over her own open mouth.

Inside the box, looking as pretty and perfect as ever, was Carrie-Ann.

'She's dead!' whispered Nancy in horror.

'I'm not sure she is,' said Alice, touching Carrie-Ann's arm. 'She's still warm. It's like she's just… suspended.'

Another box said 'Lite' and revealed a little boy that looked just like Max, but with fair hair.

'That must be Devon,' said Alice. 'He's warm, too.'

Another box, standing up against a wall, revealed the unfortunate Mrs Trott. She was frozen with an eager smile fixed upon her face, silver horn-rimmed glasses on her head.

'She messed up,' said Alice. 'So no-one is safe from them.'

The next box was even more worrying. The label said 'Bloom'. It was empty.

'Are they after me,' said Nancy. 'Or you?'

'I don't know,' said Alice. 'But either way, we're in danger.'

'You certainly are,' said a voice from the door.

The girls turned to find Nancy's mother in the open doorway.

'You two girls have both gone too far,' said Veronica Bloom. 'I have no choice but to take action. Come with me please.'

'But, mum…'

'To your room, please, Nancy. You too, Alice. Right now please.'

She escorted the girls into the house, passing the Mayor along the way. He was in the kitchen doorway in his dressing gown, holding a cup.

'Oh, Nancy,' he said, sadly. 'Look what you've done.'

'Dad?'

He shook his head and went to refill his coffee.

Veronica took the girls upstairs and to Nancy's room. Even Alice went quietly. She knew immediately that it wouldn't help their situation at all to antagonise Mrs Bloom.

Nancy was crying.

'I'm so sorry, mother. What's going to happen to us?'

'Not now. Stay here, be quiet, and don't make things worse.'

She locked the door behind her, leaving the girls together.

Alice put a comforting arm around Nancy.

'It'll be okay,' she said.

Nancy knew that was a lie, but she appreciated it nevertheless.

After what seemed like hours, Max's legs were starting to cramp and his stomach rumbled loudly.

'That's it,' he said. 'I'm getting out of here.'

He jumped up and did a few kung fu moves for good measure.

'Okay. I'm ready.'

He opened the door and came face to face with Francine La Mer.

'Dammit!'

Nancy and Alice were in the room all day. Alice had tried to unlock the door and windows, but they were stuck firm.

They were out of ideas, and worried about Max. Nancy was used to spending hours in her room, and tried to do homework or read a book to pass the time, but Alice paced up and down like a caged animal.

At lunchtime, Millicent brought them a tray with lunch on it. Veronica waited outside the door with the key.

She placed it on the table and looked at the scared girls.

'Make sure you eat,' she said. Glancing at the door, she put a hand on Nancy's. 'It'll be okay,' she whispered.

'Can you help us Millie?'

The older girl glanced at the open door again. 'I'm sorry,' she said, sadly.

Veronica locked the door again once Millie had left.

Eventually, the windows began to darken. Outside the little room, the entire village was getting ready for the competition results.

'I hope Max is okay,' said Nancy.

'He'll be okay,' said Alice. 'He's scrappy.'

'I wonder when they are going to come for us.'

Just then, the door opened, and Veronica came into the room.

She faced the two girls with a stern expression.

'What you have done,' she said,' has caused great trouble for all of you. None of the children are safe anymore.'

'Mum, what's going on?'

'I know you have your suspicions about the WI. It's true that we are different. We aren't from here. We are from another world, one where we have power to create and control life. We came here to watch and see how you live.'

'Hold on,' said Alice. 'Are you saying you are an *alien*?'

'Not exactly. We are not from another planet. We are from other worlds, worlds that exist in parallels to your own. We can move through time and space very easily.'

'That explains how you were able to live in two places at once, said Alice.

Nancy was in shocked silence. 'Do they want to hurt us? Can't you stop them?'

'I've done what I can, but it's too late,' she said, abruptly. 'They want you for dissimilation. You need to run.'

'Good,' said Alice. 'Come on.' She pulled Nancy towards the bedroom door.

'No, wait!' said Nancy. 'What's going on?'

Veronica held Nancy's hands in hers. It was the most motherly gesture she had ever shown to the girl.

'I'm so sorry,' said Veronica. 'It was never supposed to be like this. It was just a game. We just wanted to create a perfect child, and to entertain ourselves in the meantime. But now that you two have met, it has caused irrevocable damage.'

'What do you mean?'

'There is no time to explain. You are in danger. Mrs La Mer has taken things too far. I need you to get out of the way until I can find her. Please just go.'

She grabbed them each in an arm and hugged them tight. 'My girls.'

'See ya!' said Alice, pulling Nancy behind her.

'Be safe!' Veronica called after them. 'Be safe!'

Chapter Twenty-Three

The Christmas sky was filled with stars as the two girls ran through the snowy streets.

There was no-one around, except for the odd worker on their way home. Everyone else was either celebrating or getting ready to celebrate.

Nancy had on thick red furry boots that held up well on the slippy ground. Alice held onto her for support as she slid along in her wet black school shoes. Nancy liked to be needed like that, despite everything.

The stars seemed to follow them across the dark churchyard and in through the door.

Both girls stopped for a moment, blinking, as they came out of the dark entrance into the large nave of the church. Lights and candles twinkled and burned throughout the room, glittering against the highly polished brasses on the altar.

'It's beautiful,' breathed Nancy.

'Hush,' said Alice, pulling her to one side. 'They could be anywhere.'

The chapel was silent as it awaited its congregation. The girls held their breath and listened.

'I heard something,' said Alice. 'A door. Downstairs.'

'The basement! And I know how to get there!'

They went through a heavy door beside them and through several small rooms. Nancy went to a door set in the wall and pulled hard until it gave way with a scraping noise.

'How do you know your way around so well,' whispered Alice.

'I used to be a choirgirl here.'

'Of course you did.'
'What does that mean?'
'Nothing. You're just…..good.'
Nancy was still deciding whether or not to be offended when they heard someone coming from the back of the church.
Alice pushed Nancy through the door, followed quickly, and pulled it closed behind them.

Chapter Twenty-Four

The night outside was cold and wet and wild. The damp seemed to seep down through the building and permeate the cold basement.

Max sat on the hard wooden chair and watched as Mrs La Mer walked around the room, lighting candles with a long, thin stick. Her expensive shoes had heels on that made a sharp click with each step on the concrete floor.

He knew that there would soon be other people upstairs in the church, that the choir would soon be arriving, but he wasn't sure anyone would be able to hear him if he made a noise. He didn't want to risk making things worse by trying something if no-one was going to hear him anyway.

'I used to like children,' said Mrs La Mer, conversationally, as she circled him like a wild animal. 'I thought children were interesting and fun. I even wanted one or two of my own.'

She stopped in front of him. The candles burned brightly behind her, shielding her face with shadow. She was dark and fiery and demonic.

Max began to feel afraid, but he was determined not to show it. Demons like her liked that kind of thing.

'Now I know,' she said, 'that all children are trouble, all children are pests, all children are just plain naughty.'

'That's not true,' said Max, bravely. 'We are all good really, until adults change us. We don't have to be naughty inside to sometimes do naughty things.'

'Well, you're naughty inside, young Max,' she said, in a smooth hissing voice like a snake sliding through grass. 'You've caused trouble that was none of your business. You're one of the worst ones.'

'I am not,' said Max. 'You're the worst one!'

Francine La Mer started to pace around him again.

'Insolence, impudence, insubordination,' she counted off. 'Your sins are great, and can not be tolerated any longer. Many have been dissimilated for much less!'

She went over to her large black handbag in the corner and pulled out a long thin needle.

'Luckily,' she said, 'I always carry the necessary implements. Just in case.'

Max's fear was now very real. He didn't think he had ever felt quite so alone in his whole life.

Nancy and Alice had heard the noise from upstairs when Max had been grabbed and pulled down to the basement by the evil Mrs La Mer. They had quickly huddled behind a stack of wooden boxes in the corner of the basement.

Here they crouched, watching as poor Max was thrown into a chair and bullied by the nasty woman.

It was chilly in the basement. Nancy was warm in her red fuzzy jumper, but Alice only had on a thin t-shirt and a damp jacket. Nancy huddled closer to help keep Alice warm, and Alice smiled gratefully.

It was still strange to Nancy to see her own face looking back at her, but framed with all that dark hair.

Snow White and Rose Red, she thought.

Max had his back to them, so they didn't know how to let him know they were there. They didn't want to risk letting Francine know as well, or she was likely to dissimilate the lot of them.

'I have an idea,' said Alice, so quietly that Nancy wasn't sure if she'd said it out loud or in her head. She looked at Alice, who put a finger to her lips, and opened her hand.

In it was a round red sweet wrapped in plastic. A raspberry bomb, Max's favourite.

Mrs La Mer had just fished a shiny needle from her fat black bag and was holding it up to the candlelight to admire it.

'You can't do this,' Max was saying. 'You're not allowed to decide on your own. Everyone has to vote.'

'You little brat,' hissed Francine. 'Don't you dare tell me what I can and cannot do. What would you know about it anyway?'

'I know a lot,' said Max. He wondered if what he was saying was very brave or very stupid. 'I know it's you and the other women. I know about Devon.'

'Devon was a little brat, too! He deserved what he got.'

'You shouldn't say that about a child. He was only a little boy.'

'Just like you? A little meddling boy, nothing but trouble.' She moved closer. 'Now don't fight, and you won't feel a thing.'

She held the needle up to the light again, and smiled at the shiny point.

There was a noise from behind her, a clattering against stone.

She spun. 'What was that?'

Max saw something roll out onto the floor, something that had been thrown across the room.

It was a Raspberry Bomb. He'd eaten enough of them to recognise one, even in this dim light.

He looked around and saw the tip of a dark head vanish back behind a stack of boxes. Alice!

'It was a rat,' he said. 'A big one. It went over there.'

Mrs La Mer shuddered. 'Nasty creatures.' She turned back to Max. 'Speaking of which…'

'Shouldn't you wait for the rest of the women?' he said, again. 'They will be here soon. Then you can kill me with an easy conscience.'

Mrs La Mer looked surprised. Her thin witchy face actually softened a little.

'Kill?' she said. 'Who said anything about kill? It's just a little procedure.'

'I saw the others,' he said, trying to buy time. ' Carrie-Ann and Mrs Trott and the others. She messed up, didn't she? Mrs Trott? She nearly let the secret out, didn't she? So you killed her.'

If there was anything he had learned from films and books, it was that the bad guy liked to confess all just before they killed, they liked to brag about what they had done.

'What did Devon do?' he said, taunting her. 'Did he call you out on your evil plans? Your mean old women's group?'

'The WI is a wonderful thing,' said Mrs La Mer. 'Through meetings and coffee mornings, we can quite literally put the world to rights.'

Alice and Nancy watched all of this, breathless. Max seemed to have taken strength from knowing they were there, but he was obviously buying them time so they could do something. The only problem was, they had no idea what to do.

'The WI,' he scoffed. 'What is that anyway? Witches International?'

To his surprise, Francine laughed.

'Close,' she said. 'Actually, it stands for Watchers Inter-dimensional.' She raised the needle. 'We aren't like you, young Max. We don't let the world dictate to us. We dictate to the world.'

She leaned over him, and he squeezed back into the chair as far as he could go.

'You can't do this,' he said.'

'Oh, yes, I can. You see, you are nothing. Just an social experiment. I created you and I can take you away. We made you as part of a game, a competition to create the perfect child. We created you all. It seems that in your case, we failed.'

'Wow,' mouthed Alice to Nancy, wide-eyed. 'Plot twist!'

'I suppose you could equate it to a reality TV show, that trash that everyone watches these days. We grew bored, so we decided to make children and put them in different lives - rich ones, poor ones, loved ones, neglected ones - just to see how they would turn out.

'We can't have children, you see, but we are able to make anything we want to. For each child we created, we made a clone, or twin. It is called Assimilation. Each twin would be placed in a different family situation, with families that couldn't have children. They were happy to agree to the terms. People will do anything when they long for a child.

'We pitted the twins against each other, without their knowledge. Behaviour, achievements, friendships. Every now and then, we got together - at one of out famed coffee mornings - to revise the situation. Those children who were failing were removed from the contest. It is called Dissimilation. They were shut down, so to speak.'

'You mean killed?'

'No, no, not killed. It is a state of sleep. We can wake them at any time, but why would we want to?'

'Why did you put the children in villages so close together. Didn't you think we would meet?'

'Well, that is where we were mistaken. We saw that the rich and poor do not ever mix. We assumed that snobbery would keep you apart. Unfortunately, it didn't, and they all turned out just like you. They all went bad. The experiment failed.'

She advanced with the needle.

'Now hold still for just a moment. It's just a slight scratch to the back of the neck and all your troubles will be gone.'

As she stepped over him, Max panicked and kicked out so hard that his chair overturned and he landed hard on the floor on his back.

Nancy and Alice looked at each other in fear. It was time to do something, anything.

The witch leapt on him. 'Keep still, you little brat. You're going to ruin everything. I just wanted to create the perfect child.'

The girls leapt up from their hiding place. 'You already have,' Nancy shouted.

'Twice,' said Alice.

Chapter Twenty-Five

Despite the warmth of the many candles that surrounded the church congregation, and the huddled bodies of the congregation itself, Marguerite felt a chill go right through her.

In the row in front of her, little Joey Litten turned and grinned at her. He pulled an ugly face, then an even uglier one. His mother spotted him and swatted him round the head until he stopped.

Turning slowly, Marguerite looked around the room. Millie, sitting across the aisle, was staring at her.

She looked for her mother, but couldn't see her anywhere. A man and woman burst in the back door, looking worried, but didn't come any further. She saw Nancy's mother, checking her watch.

Mayor Bloom was sitting up front with the representatives of other villages. An old man who looked like a skinny Santa was sitting beside him, looking very uncomfortable and shifting in his seat.

Millie caught her eye again. She was still watching her. Millie shook her head briefly.

The vicar was heading to the podium by the altar, about to speak.

Marguerite stood suddenly.

People in the nearby rows looked at her, expectantly. Marguerite flushed, not sure what she was doing. She quickly moved along the row, excusing herself to those whose knees she budged or feet she stood on.

As she headed to the back of the church, Millie slipped out of her aisle seat and caught up with her.

'What are you doing?' hissed Mille.

'I don't know. Something's wrong.'

'Stay out of it. It's too dangerous.'

Marguerite looked at the older girl closely for the first time. Sweet, kind Millicent, who had always been there to look after them. There was a fire in her green eyes that Marguerite had never seen before.

'What do you know?'

'Nothing. Sit down. I'll go.'

'Where's my mother?'

'I don't know.'

'You're lying,' said the timid Marguerite, surprised. 'Why are you lying?'

The vicar took to the podium and the couple by the door hustled into seats at the back.

Marguerite ran for the side door, closely followed by Millie.

They didn't realise that Veronica Bloom had seen their every move and was poised to follow.

'Good? GOOD?'

Francine La Mer had recovered quickly from her surprise at seeing both Bloom girls in one place, and her anger had returned in spades.

'You? Good?'

She rounded on Alice.

'You little wench. You're the worst one! You lie, you steal, you cheat, you skip school! What kind of child are you to say you are good? Do your parents work day and night for this?'

'I'm not doing those things anymore,' said Alice, defiantly. 'I've changed.'

'Oh, so Naughty Alice has changed her spots, has she?' said Francine, confusing her English sayings in her rage. 'You have been the biggest failure yet!'

She loomed over the little girl. Her voice became gentle and sickly sweet. 'One sharp little scratch and we can put an end to your parents' misery,' she cooed. 'They will be so much happier without you, you know. They can't afford someone like you, ungrateful, greedy girl.' She held out her fingernails toward Alice's throat as though they were needles themselves. Alice stared at her wide-eyed, as though hypnotised.

It's true, thought Alice. *My mum and dad deserve a good life. They can't afford to have me. I'm nothing but a burden. If I love them, I'll go away. Just one little scratch....*

'Alice, no!' screamed Nancy, as Mrs La Mer's shadow loomed large on the wall behind them, her sharp claws ready.

All of a sudden, a lot of things happened at once.

Chapter Twenty-Six

Nancy screamed, and at the same time, Max leapt up and right onto Mrs La Mer's back.

She shrieked and tried to shake him off, but he clung tight around her neck.

'Hold onto her!' yelled Alice, as she went for the needle. She wrestled with the woman until Francine dropped the needle and grabbed Alice instead.

Nancy went for the locked door and started to bang and scream for help.

Alice scooped up the needle and jabbed it into the woman's arm till she let go of her.

Yelling like a banshee, Francine flung herself backwards, crushing little Max between herself and a pile of boxes.

Max, Francine and the boxes all tumbled to the ground.

One of the boxes landed between them and fell open, and the frozen body of Mrs Blatch rolled out.

The children screamed with shock.

'She killed her!' shouted Max.'

At the same time, the door flew open and Millicent came inside.

Francine was back on her feet, snarling and dishevelled.

'What the hell do you want?' she sneered at Millie.

'Let the children go,' said Millie.

'You don't ever DARE tell me what to do!' hissed Francine. 'I am in charge here.'

'Not any more.'

'I knew I should have got rid of you when I had the chance. You were always worse than Jennifer. As usual, our dear Veronica stepped in and saved you, sacrificing your sister. She always did have her favourites.'

Millie's lip shook. 'You're mean,' she spat. 'You're mean and evil and cruel. You took a simple game and you turned it into a vehicle for your own viciousness.'

'Oh, shut up, you stupid little girl.'

'Hey, don't you talk to Millie like that!' shouted Nancy, surprising even herself. 'She's good and she's kind and she's everything you're not.'

'Oh, spare me,' said Francine. 'You brats make me sick.'

She grabbed Max by the arm he hurt earlier and yanked him to his feet.

'Now everyone shut up and sit down, or I'll kill the boy.'

Max was trying hard not to cry out, but tears of pain crept from his big dark eyes and down his grimy little face.

'Leave him alone,' said Alice.'

Francine grinned and pulled Max's arm even higher, so that he had to go up onto his tiptoes to try to ease the pain.

'Now who's in charge?' she purred.

'I am,' said Veronica from the doorway. Behind her were Martha and Kennedy.

'Mum!' said Nancy.

'Mum! Dad!' said Alice. 'I'm so sorry!' She had never in her whole life been so relieved to see her parents.

'Mrs La Mer, put down the child,' said Veronica Bloom.

'I'm afraid not,' said Francine. 'I'm calling the contest. I win. Getting rid of these awful children will be my prize.'

'Quite the contrary, Francine. You are disqualified, from the game, and from the Wives Institute It's over. So is the Wives Institute'

'I beg to disagree.'

Mrs La Mer yanked harder on Max's arm and he called out in agony. Alice couldn't bear it any longer. She raced forward and pulled Max away from her.

The two of them landed in the pile of boxes.

In a second, Francine reached out and got hold of Nancy by her hair. She pulled the needle from her own arm and held it up in a stabbing position at the back of Nancy's neck.

Alice and Max scrabbled toward the door and were pulled to safety by Alice's parents.

'No!' shouted Veronica.

'Well, well, well,' smiled Francine. 'We seem to have ourselves a little stand-off.'

'Don't hurt my daughter,' said Veronica.

'I'll tell you what,' Francine said. 'I'll trade her for you.'

'No!' said Nancy. 'Mum, no!'

'Yes,' agreed Veronica. 'Just please let her go.'

Francine threw Nancy behind her and she hit the wall, hard, landing heavy on the ground.

'Kneel down,' Francine commanded of Veronica. 'It is time for your dissimilation.'

Veronica looked at Nancy. 'I'm so sorry,' she said. 'This was all my fault.'

'Yes, yes, very moving. Now KNEEL.'

Veronica dropped to her knees and lowered her head, as Francine triumphantly raised the needle above her.

Nancy was about to scream, when a small door in the wall beside her opened silently and someone came through it with a finger to their lips.

Nancy watched breathlessly as the person crept up behind Francine.

'I'm sorry, Veronica,' said Francine, smugly. 'I wish it didn't have to end this way.'

She made to lower the needle point into Veronica's neck, then stopped, her eyes wide, her mouth open in shock. She dropped to the ground with a crash.

Behind her, Marguerite stood crying, a needle in her hand. It was Veronica's, given to Millie earlier that day, then given to Marguerite in the corridor before they split up, Millie to the basement door, and Marguerite to the tunnel that led to the old Priest's hole.

Nancy wasn't the only one who had been an altar girl.

'Now, it's over,' said Marguerite. Veronica stood and held the girl, and then Nancy who ran into her arms.

'I'll fix this,' said Veronica. 'It was a stupid, harmful game. I see that now. I'll find a way to wake them up, all of them.'

She looked down at Francine's body.

'Well, most of them.'

The weary battlers made their way back up into the brightly lit church. The congregation had dispersed apart from a few stragglers and the competition organisers.

Mayor Bloom came rushing over to check on his wife and daughter, barely acknowledging Alice and her family, who stood beside them.

Millie had taken Max to look for a first aider to check on his arm and see if it was broken.

'This is your fault,' said Martha to Veronica, angrily. 'You took advantage of our desire to have a child. Alice is our daughter and we love her. She isn't a pawn in your sick game.'

'I love Nancy too. I did everything I could to protect them both.'

'Except for creating this problem in the first place!'

'I accept it was wrong, and it won't happen again. We just want to live among you quietly, and help where we can.'

'Now, now, ladies,' boomed the Mayor in his most disarming manner. 'We can all see where the problems began. It is indeed a man's world, but it was created by a woman.'

The two women rounded on the Mayor.

'What does that mean?' demanded Martha.

'For goodness' sake, Horatio,' said his wife. 'None of this would have happened at all if you hadn't turned your back on your family in Hogweed Fields. Your snobbery is what gave us the idea in the first place!'

'You're from Hogweed Fields?' said Kennedy, surprised. 'Are we related?'

The two men faced each other.

'I'm afraid so. Your dad Hilary was my brother. When he passed away, the business came to me. I'm the owner of Franklin's garage. Franklin was my dad. We all have quite heroic names, you see. He was like that.'

'So you're the one running me out of business, blocking the roads, raising the rent?'

Kennedy wondered whether or not he should punch the Mayor right here in front of everyone.

'I owe you an apology,' said Horacio. 'I had no right to treat you the way I did. Sometimes I get carried away, and forget to think about how those things might affect other people. It just always felt so good to win.'

'I wouldn't know. I've never won a thing in my life,' said Kennedy. 'I'm still a lucky man, though. I have a family I love, and a good job, and we have a home. That's more than a lot of people have.'

'You'll have much more from now on,' said the Mayor. 'I have been a terrible landlord. That will change from now on. After all, we are family.'

They shook hands, embarrassed.

Alice and Nancy hugged each other. It made them so happy to see their families together like this.

It was almost worth it all.

Just then, Max came running over to them, his arm in a makeshift sling.

'We won,' he screamed at Alice.

'What?'

'The Christmas competition! We won!'

'What? How?'

'They loved us, and they loved George. He took the lead in everything while we were gone.'

Alice looked at her parents. 'Is that true?'

They nodded, smiling.

'Ah, yes,' said the Mayor. 'I forgot to offer you my congratulations. The River County organisers were very impressed with the whole village effort put in by Hogweed Fields. Apparently, the spirit of community and charity were exactly what they were looking for.'

'Yes!' yelled Alice. 'In your face! Boom!'

She whooped with joy, then notice everyone looking at her.

'I mean, thank you,' she said, politely, smiling sweetly at the Mayor. 'You're right. It does feel good to win.'

Chapter Twenty-Seven

A month later, the new Hogweed Fields playground was completed and Alice and her friends spent many happy hours there when they weren't in school.
The £50,000 had gone a long way in the village. Much of it had gone to the cafe, who had been able to install an outreach program. To begin with, Alice's mother had taken Christmas dinner and gifts to every family that needed it. The cafe was doing so well that they needed extra help, so she had employed George on a part-time basis and had made up a room for him to live in out the back. After all, his wonderful performance as Santa Claus had charmed the competition judges no end.
A clothing fund had been set up for the poorer families, and extra money was available to help pay for uniforms, books and school trips.
Franklin's garage was doing equally as well, thanks to Mayor Bloom. The Mayor had asked Alice's father to join him in the family business as a 50/50 partner. Horatio provided the money and Kennedy did the work. With the extortionate rents of previous years, the business flourished and provided apprenticeships for school leavers.
For Alice, though, the best change was in Max. He was now living with the Blooms on a foster basis, and was doing very well outside of his parent's negative influence. He went to school every day, as did Alice, and he had even joined the scouts. Sometimes on Saturdays he went to the garage and Kennedy gave him a few pounds pocket money for helping out, which made Max feel very proud.

'I promised I wouldn't ditch you after all this was over,' Alice told him the day he moved in. At first there were a few teething troubles with sharing a room, but the Blooms were hoping to move to somewhere with a little more space one day soon.

On Christmas Eve, the family had gone for dinner at the Manor. Mayor Bloom was in his element showing off the house to his new-found relations, and Alice and Max had loved the limo ride over there.

Alice and Nancy had been overjoyed to find that they were related, but still thought of themselves as sisters, which technically they were.
A friendship between Sunny Meadows and Hogweed Fields had sprung from the family connections, and from the shame the Mayor felt for having forgotten his roots for such a long time.

The Mayor had thrown a big party for all the children in the Winter Wonderland, with fairground rides and lots of good food. No-one had to sneak in the back, and the Hogweed Fields children walked in the front with their new Sunny Meadows friends. And, as promised, there were real reindeers.

One late January day, the limo coasted down the narrow streets of Hogweed Fields on the way to visit the cafe, which the Mayor now supported generously from his own pocket. He even did the dishes once, but he didn't do them very well, and he dramatically got his cufflink caught in the waste disposal, so his further offers were politely declined.

The children were all out playing on the new playground on a mild and sunshiney day.

Nancy saw them from the car window.

'Can't I go and play just for a minute?' she asked, hopefully.

Veronica looked at the damp ground and the children with their grubby knees, then at Nancy's new maroon boots.

'No, of course not, dear…'

Mayor Bloom leaned forward and put a hand on his wife's knee.

'Let's all go, shall we?' he said.

Chester pulled up alongside the grass and the Blooms got out of the car. Nancy looked at her parents.

'Go on then,' smiled her father.

Across the grass, Alice saw them and waved.

Nancy ran across the field toward her twin. She turned and waved happily at her watching parents, before running with Alice to the spinning roundabout filled with gleeful children. She leapt aboard and laughed along with them, her hair flying freely in the wind.

'Horatio, what if she falls off,' said her worried mother.

'Then she'll get back on.' He put an arm around his wife's shoulder. 'She only has a few more years of being a child. Let her enjoy them.'

They walked slowly over the grass towards the playing children.

'I'm so sorry, Horatio,' said Veronica. 'All this has been my fault. Do you ever wish you had made a different turn that day and not come to Sunny Meadows, after all?'

'Of course not,' said Mayor Bloom. 'I wouldn't change a thing.'

Printed in Great Britain
by Amazon